Kim Lawrence is a rising star in Modern Romance™. Her fast-paced, exciting stories, packed full of sizzling attraction and laugh-out-loud moments, will whisk you away!

Praise for **Kim Lawrence**

About BABY AND THE BOSS:

'Ms Lawrence's tale has great character rapport, charming scenes and strong chemistry.'
—*Romantic Times*

About A CONVENIENT HUSBAND:

'Kim Lawrence's layered conflict creates an emotional tale about strong characters.'
—*Romantic Times*

Kim Lawrence lives on a farm in rural Anglesey. She runs two miles daily and finds this an excellent opportunity to unwind and seek inspiration for her writing! It also helps her keep up with her husband, two active sons, and the various stray animals which have adopted them. Always a fanatical consumer of fiction, she is now equally enthusiastic about writing. She loves a happy ending!

Recent titles by the same author:

THE GROOM'S ULTIMATUM
THE BLACKMAILED BRIDE
THE PROSPECTIVE WIFE
A CONVENIENT HUSBAND
A SEDUCTIVE REVENGE

THE GREEK TYCOON'S WIFE

BY

KIM LAWRENCE

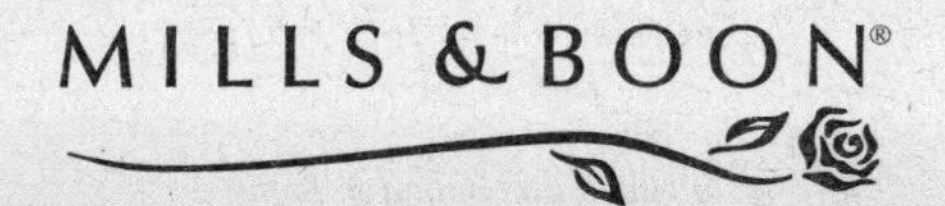

First published in Great Britain 2002
Harlequin Mills & Boon Limited,
Eton House, 18-24 Paradise Road, Richmond, Surrey TW9 1SR

ISBN 0 263 83200 7

Set in Times Roman 10½ on 11¼ pt.
01-0103-51365

Printed and bound in Spain
by Litografia Rosés, S.A., Barcelona

CHAPTER ONE

ONLY the privileged few ever got to see the top floor of the towering glass edifice that was the Lakis Building, and entry to the boardroom was even more exclusive. It therefore came as something of a shock to the élite few gathered there when the big double doors crashed open in the middle of a board meeting.

Nikos Lakis, silver shards of annoyance filtering into his dark almond-shaped eyes, opened his mouth to deliver a devastating reprimand, then closed it again as the identity of the intruder was revealed.

The attractive redhead strode into the room and planted her hands on her curvy hips just as Nikos's breathless PA appeared behind her. The younger woman rolled her eyes and shrugged apologetically towards her boss before retreating post-haste.

'Well!' There was a long dramatic pause, timed to perfection, before Caitlin Lakis delivered her punchline.

It was worth the build-up.

'Is it true, Nik? Are you actually planning to marry *that* woman? Have you lost your mind...?'

Caitlin didn't actually expect her stepson to defend his actions or lack of them to her. In her experience Greek men in general were not prone to explaining themselves and the Lakis men in particular.

The individual these scathing accusations were aimed at appeared to be the only person around the long table who was not excruciatingly embarrassed by the attack. During the pulsating pause that followed his stepmother's heated harangue Nikos sat there calmly rotating the pen he held between his long brown fingers.

'If nobody has any objections...?'

The suited figures he addressed showed no inclination to object, most would sooner have leapt from the twentieth-floor plate-glass window that revealed the city below than disagree with him. Two years earlier they had been reluctantly prepared to accept his presence just because of who his father was, most had not thought he would last long.

Now the respect they gave him was based on the fact they knew he delivered the goods. The playboy had turned out to have a brain like a steel trap and nerves to match. He gave his all and expected those around him to do no less.

'Then I think that's it for today. Thank you, gentlemen.'

The board members got to their feet with alacrity.

'How is Father?'

'Your father is fine. Don't change the subject,' Caitlin retorted. 'I'm waiting.'

Nikos appeared more amused than dismayed by this stern pronouncement as, one dark brow raised, his glance slid significantly towards the men who were hurriedly gathering their belongings.

Though she looked irritated, Caitlin managed to restrain herself until the door closed behind the last of the board members; she even responded politely to several stilted enquiries after her health.

A flicker of amusement slid into Nikos's silver-shot eyes as he watched her efforts to contain her frustration. The woman who had married his father some eighteen years earlier had many virtues, but patience wasn't one of them. Though he conceded Caitlin had been patient enough when it had come to gaining the trust of her suspicious stepsons.

He could recall the exact moment she had won him over. He still couldn't decide if her display of ignorance and panic when faced with a table groaning with antique silver and priceless porcelain had been genuine or just for his benefit.

'It doesn't really matter what fork you use,' he'd explained. 'Just act like you know what you're doing and people will think they've got it wrong.'

For a full sixty seconds Caitlin had stared at the twelve-year-old before shaking her head and exclaiming, 'That could have been your father talking.'

Nikos had felt a warm glow at her words.

'You must be thinking of Dimitri.' Dimitri the favoured eldest, was being groomed to take over from his father.

'Dimitri looks like Spyros,' Caitlin conceded. 'But you...' she tapped her head '...think like him...'

Now the owner of her own successful fashion business, Caitlin, an extremely attractive forty-five, didn't look so very much different as she had done back then.

'Right, they've gone,' she said briskly the moment the big double doors closed. 'Though I think it's a bit late for discretion. Since I got to Athens that's all I've been hearing...*when is the wedding?*' She gave a snort. 'You can't tell me you're in love with Livia Nikolaidis.'

'What's love?'

Caitlin rolled her eyes and clicked her tongue at this blatant piece of provocation. 'So you've had a couple of bad experiences...who hasn't?' she snapped unsympathetically. 'So kindly spare me the weary cynicism and stop avoiding the issue, Nik.'

Nikos accepted the reprimand with a rueful grin.

Caitlin might be his stepmother, but she was female and her stern expression briefly softened perceptively.

Even as she tartly observed, 'You should smile more,' she privately conceded he maybe didn't have that much time or reason to smile since the responsibilities of the entire Lakis empire had fallen on his shoulders. No matter how broad those shoulders might be—in Nikos's case, enough for two average men.

'I'm not in love with Livia,' he admitted calmly.

Being in love with Livia might have been an obstacle to their successful union, because if he'd been in love he wouldn't have been able to see that though Livia was beautiful and accomplished she was also extremely selfish and terminally vain. This way he had no unreasonable expectations of her that might later disappoint him. And Livia, being a product of a background very similar to his own, would not make unreasonable demands on him and his time.

Caitlin gave a deep sigh of relief. 'Then it's not true, you haven't been seeing her…'

'Did I say that? Many women fantasise about marrying a rich man…'

'My, you do have a high opinion of my sex.'

Nikos acknowledged his stepmother's dig with a shrug. 'I can only speak from my own experience.'

'Which is wide and varied…' Despite the disapproval in her tone Caitlin didn't find it particularly surprising that her stepson had gained this jaundiced perspective of women. From the moment he hit puberty girls *and* women had been drawn to him like a magnet and he was selling himself short if he thought his wealth was the only thing they were after.

'The reality of marriage to the man who is responsible for the day to day running of the Lakis business is something which many women couldn't handle.'

'I did,' Caitlin reminded him. The severity of her expression softened. 'With a little help from my friends.'

'You are an exceptional woman. Livia is not exceptional, but she is born to the life. I think Livia and I might suit very well.'

Caitlin stared at him, horrified; it seemed there was nothing more humourless or stupid than a reformed playboy. *'Oh, my God…!'*

'I take it you don't like Livia,' Nikos observed, smiling in an indulgent manner his stepmother found extremely provocative.

'My liking her has nothing whatever to do with it.'

Nikos raised one eloquent winged brow.

'Well, maybe a bit,' his stepmother conceded, thinking of the perfectly groomed brunette with the calculating smile and the hard eyes. As she worriedly scanned her handsome stepson's face her antagonism slipped away, leaving an expression of deep concern. 'Nik, darling, she's all wrong for you. You *can't* marry her.'

'That's true, I can't—not while I'm already married.'

His stepmother fell gracefully off her chair.

'Wow, what a rock!' Sadie breathed, catching hold of her friend's small hand before she could hide it beneath the table. She blinked as the diamond, which seemed almost too heavy for the younger girl's finger, caught the light. 'It's gorgeous,' she said enviously. 'Though I have to admit,' she mused, lifting her eyes to Katie's slightly flushed face, 'I'd have thought you'd have gone for something a little less…'

'Flashy…?' Katie responded without thinking. She frowned to hear the wistful edge in her voice. There was just no pleasing some people, she chided herself irritably.

'Less…conventional,' Sadie contradicted tactfully. 'Something to go with your charity-shop bargains. It's so unfair, I spend more on clothes in a week than you do in a year and look at me!' she invited gloomily. 'Maybe if I didn't eat for a month clothes would look like that on me…' With an envious sigh she examined her friend's tall, effortlessly slender figure. 'No, that wouldn't work—I'd end up with even smaller boobs than I already have!'

She eyed the younger girl's well-defined bosom with good-natured resentment and then philosophically bit into the last cream cake on the plate.

Katie's thoughts drifted as she sat looking at her finger, thinking a little wistfully of the ruby ring set with seed pearls she'd seen in the window of a small antique shop.

The one Tom had seemed to quite like until he had got a look at the modest price tag; then he had dismissed it as a pretty trifle not worthy of consideration.

'You pay for quality,' he explained patiently as they left the shop empty-handed. 'What a peculiar girl you are,' he added with a perplexed expression on his open, good-looking face. 'Tell most girls price is no object and they'd head for the most expensive jewellers in town. I'm not a mean man, sweetheart.'

'I know that. In fact you're *too* generous, Tom.' A frown pleated Katie's broad, smooth forehead. Tom just wasn't able to accept the fact that she would have been just as happy with an inexpensive token as the extravagant gifts he showered her with.

'Well, once we're married you'll have to get used to it,' Tom announced. 'You're a beautiful woman, you deserve beautiful things, and I,' he told her firmly, 'am going to make sure you get them. Whether you like it or not,' he added with a determined grin.

'But all I want is you, Tom,' she told him earnestly.

Tom looked startled and then pleased as he drew her to his side. *'Really...?'*

'Of course really.' Katie was uneasily aware that she sounded like someone trying to convince herself. 'I guess I'm just not a very...demonstrative person,' she admitted regretfully.

'I've told you I don't mind waiting,' he told her quietly. 'I admire your principles, darling.'

Principles or just a low sex drive...?

Katie ignored the vexatious voice in her head and reminded herself how incredibly lucky she was to have discovered such a sensitive, understanding man who loved her to distraction.

But not so much distraction that he can't keep his hands off you... Katie muttered to herself.

With extra warmth she pressed a soft kiss to Tom's lips.

After all, why would you want to be with a man who would be unable to restrain his base animal urges…? The sarcastic voice in her head just had to have the last word.

'Tom really liked this one,' she told her friend.

'That figures.' Sadie bit her lip and looked apologetic. 'Sorry, love, but you have to admit he does operate on a strict "if you've got it, flaunt it" policy.'

Katie sighed. 'I know, but he means well, Sadie, and he really is the *kindest* man I've ever met,' she told the older girl earnestly.

And dull as ditch water! 'So it's official now.'

For six months Tom Percival had pursued Katie with single-minded determination.

Sadie balanced her chin on her steepled fingers. 'So how did he take it when you told him?'

Katie took a sip of her tea; her grimace wasn't because the liquid was hot. 'Well, actually…' she began, avoiding eye contact.

Sadie gasped. 'You *did* tell him…?'

Katie's shoulders hunched defensively as Sadie's shocked response reinforced her guilt. 'He was so happy and I was waiting for the right moment.' It sounded a pathetically lame excuse even to her own ears.

Sadie groaned so loudly that half the people in the tea shop turned around to look at them. 'When would be a better time—at the altar?' she croaked, gazing at the younger woman incredulously. 'Listen, I'd be the first to agree that what happened before he came along is none of his business, a girl's skeletons are her affair, but you're still *married*, love. That does sort of make it relevant.'

'I know…I know!' Katie closed her eyes and twisted her fingers. 'I just don't *feel* married. I was *going* to tell him…I *will* tell him, but I might as well wait now until I hear back from Harvey.'

'Harvey's the lawyer who brokered the marriage deal?'

Katie nodded.

'He sounds a bit shady to me.'

Hearing the very proper and fairly prim Harvey Reynolds, QC described this way made Katie smile; she felt she had to defend his good name.

'Well, he isn't, he's one of the top criminal lawyers in the country. I've known him since I was a little girl.' She caught her full lower lip between her teeth and gnawed gently on the soft pink flesh. 'I can't see that there will be any problem getting a quickie divorce...?'

Sadie's eyebrows lifted to a satirical angle. 'I'm probably not the best person to be asking about amicable divorces,' she responded drily.

'It's not like it was a real marriage or anything.' Surely that made a difference.

'Have you *really* not seen him since the ceremony?'

Katie shook her head, she wasn't surprised at the incredulity in her friend's voice. Who wouldn't be shocked about someone marrying a total stranger? Heck, she was herself. Sometimes it seemed to her as if it had happened to someone else.

'No, not for seven years. My only link is Harvey. It always was.' The assistance of her mother's patient, but ultimately unsuccessful admirer had only been forthcoming when Katie had convinced him that she would go ahead with her plan with or without his help.

'If you're thinking about recruiting someone whose visa is running out and wants to stay in the country, forget it,' Harvey had told her in the plush surrounding of his City chambers. 'Unless, that is, you *want* to expose yourself to criminal prosecution.' He pushed his metal-framed half-moon glasses up his thin nose and looked at her severely.

'I hadn't thought of that,' Katie admitted with wide-eyed dismay.

'Seems to me you haven't thought much at all.'

'If you're going to try and stop me...'

'If I thought I had any chance of succeeding I would,'

the legal brain admitted with engaging candour. 'For your mother's sake I want to make sure you think this thing through properly—if such a thing is possible?'

'She was very fond of you too.'

Poor Harvey; there had only ever been one man for her mother and she had given up everything to be with him. Katie had wondered whether she'd ever find a love like that—one that didn't think of consequences, one that lasted for ever. She wasn't actually sure she wanted to. The idea of falling victim to such a blind, relentless passion was actually rather scary.

'You do appreciate that it's very unlikely that the sort of man who would marry you for a one-off payment would be satisfied with that?'

'How do you mean?'

'I mean there's a strong possibility that a man like that would have questionable scruples. He'd be back for more,' Harvey explained bluntly. 'And then there's the question of making yourself vulnerable to blackmail.'

'But there won't be any money, I'm giving the rest away.' Katie couldn't help but think that dealing with hardened criminals had made Harvey a little overly suspicious.

'That's another thing—is it really wise to give up your *entire* inheritance too?'

'Non-negotiable,' Kate interrupted abruptly.

'In that case—' the lawyer sighed '—how do you feel about raising the amount you'd pay the groom?'

'By how much?'

Harvey told her and she gasped. 'You've got to be kidding…?'

'It might seem a lot, well, actually it is a lot,' he conceded. 'But in the long run I really think this is your safest bet. As it happens I know of a person who needs an injection of cash and for reasons I can't go into he prefers not to approach the usual sources…'

'Five hundred thousand pounds is quite a big injection,' she began doubtfully.

'True, but the capital left over would still be more than enough to provide a very generous income for the Grahams, and there would be no question of this man ever demanding anything else of you or troubling you in any way. I'd personally guarantee that.'

'Why does this man need so much money?' she asked bluntly.

'I'm really not at liberty to discuss that, the choice is yours. All I can say is that I will *personally* guarantee this person's integrity.'

Even if this man was shady, what were her alternatives? She could advertise in a personal column but, Harvey was right, what sort of weirdos would respond to an ad for a husband?

'All right, then.'

'Excellent. All I have to do now is persuade N...him...'

'Persuade *him*...?'

'Don't worry, dear, I'm sure he'll come around,' Harvey soothed.

He had come around and up until now Katie had had no reason to regret her decision.

'So this man you married, he could be anywhere, doing anything...he might even be dead. Oh, that would be convenient.'

Her friend's joking words jolted Katie back to the present. *'Sadie!'*

Sadie grinned sheepishly. 'Well, it would. I'm just being practical.'

'I want to divorce the man, not put out a contract on him!'

Sadie normally respected the younger girl's reserve but at that moment her curiosity got the better of her. 'So all you know about this man is his name?'

Katie had never elaborated beyond saying that marriage

had been the only way she'd been able to inherit the money from her Greek grandfather's estate. Which begged the question why was Katie flat broke these days?

Katie nodded. 'Nikos Lakis.' She found herself strangely reluctant to say the name.

'Is he Greek?'

'I assumed so.'

'Nikos Lakis…mmm. Did he look as sexy as he sounds?' Sadie giggled huskily. 'Or was he short, fat and balding?'

'I can't remember,' Kate replied shortly. She wasn't quite sure why she lied. Many of her memories of that day were hazy, but not the face of the man she had stood beside and exchanged solemn vows with.

She didn't know what she'd been expecting but it hadn't been Nikos Lakis.

Harvey, watching her face anxiously as the tall Greek had arrived, must have seen the spasm of shock that had passed over her features.

'I suppose there is a little resemblance to your brother,' he murmured, intuitively sensing the source of her distress. 'I should have said…'

Katie shook her head. 'He's not really like him.'

She wasn't just saying this to make Harvey feel better. Peter's face had been extremely attractive, but stood next to this man he would have been invisible. Her twin hadn't possessed the sheer physical presence that this stranger had in abundance.

As the stranger she was about to marry inclined his dark head in acknowledgement of Harvey and turned his attention briefly to her, Katie saw there was none of Peter's petulance in this austerely beautiful face, nor any of the warmth. In fact, she saw as he came closer that he wasn't anything like her twin at all.

This man was ice.

Seven years later she was helpless to control the little shudder that slipped down her spine or the nervous flutter in her tummy as she visualised those silver-shot midnight-dark eyes fringed by decadently dark lashes set in an otherwise starkly uncompromising bronzed face.

Even if he hadn't been an attention-grabbing six feet five of solid bone and muscle and moved with the natural grace of a top-class athlete, who could forget those eyes…? She hadn't. They'd even featured in some disturbingly erotic dreams that had disrupted her sleep over the years.

'He's alive.'

Sadie raised her eyebrows at her friend's emphatic tone.

'Actually I've never seen anybody quite *so* alive.' His vitality had been like an electric current. His brief touch had made her skin tingle and she'd been relieved he hadn't prolonged the contact more than absolutely necessary.

'I thought you couldn't remember what he looked like.' Sadie watched the distant, almost dreamy expression cross the younger woman's face.

'I can't, it was just an impression,' Katie replied a little quickly, too stubborn to admit even to herself the impact her bought bridegroom had made on her.

'Quite a coincidence you both being Greek.'

Katie's soft lips firmed and her eyes filled with scorn. 'I'm *half* Greek.'

It was a half that showed in the contours of her oval face with its proud, high forehead, straight classical nose, delicately sculpted lips and long, swan-like neck. It was also a half she was always ready to deny. The half that had heartlessly cast off the daughter who had offended their precious family honour.

Not even after her husband had died and she'd been left to bring up two young children on the small salary she'd earned working part-time as a legal secretary had Katie's mother tried to contact her family who had rejected her on her wedding day.

Katie and her twin had been brought up with very little

knowledge of their mother's culture, which suited Katie fine. She had no time for people who could punish a woman for falling in love outside her class and culture. No, as far as she was concerned she was all British.

CHAPTER TWO

KEPT late by an unexpected emergency at work, Katie rang Tom to arrange to go directly to the hotel where they were having dinner. She dashed home, fed the cat, a particularly evil-tempered ginger tom called Alexander, and got changed in record time. As she emerged from the taxi nothing about her demeanour hinted at the breathless haste with which she'd got ready.

High heels crunching on the gravel, Katie hurried across the forecourt unable to dismiss the nagging feeling she had forgotten something. Walking into the brightly lit foyer, she smoothed down her freshly washed hair, which she hadn't had the time to blow-dry properly; it fell river-straight almost to her waist, gleaming like the finest spun silk under the bright lights, which picked out the rich chestnut highlights in the deep glossy brown strands.

Tom was waiting. His face lit up as she appeared and his obvious pleasure made Katie glad she had decided to wear the dress Sadie had given her with a plea for her to make use of it.

Tom kissed her hard on the mouth, which was surprising; he was normally quite undemonstrative in public. 'You look beautiful!' he said huskily as they drew apart.

'You sound surprised…' Her teasing hid a secret worry. Was it entirely normal to be thinking about whether you'd remembered to unlock the cat flap while you were being passionately kissed by the man you were going to marry? 'It must be the dress.' Though he never openly criticised the way she dressed, Katie knew he would have liked her to dress up more.

'I didn't even notice the dress,' Tom replied huskily.

'Well, there's not a lot to notice, is there?' she responded, glancing uncertainly down at the midnight-blue slip dress that clung to the soft curves of her body a little too lovingly for her comfort. 'You don't think it's a bit… *obvious*?'

The appeal made Tom throw back his head and laugh. 'You couldn't look anything but cool and classy if you tried, and I'm the luckiest man in the world.'

He might not think so soon.

Katie took a deep breath. There was never going to be a good time to tell him this, so now, she reasoned, was as good a time as any other.

'Tom, there's something I need to tell you,' she told him urgently.

A flicker of impatience crossed her fiancé's boyishly handsome features. 'We'll talk about it later, sweetheart,' he said, grabbing her hand. 'We're late as it is, and Nikos isn't used to people keeping him waiting.'

The name was so unexpected it hit her like a blow, snatching the air from her lungs and the thoughts from her head. There was a loud whooshing noise in her ears and it took several heart-thudding seconds before the room stopped spinning.

'Nikos…?' she faltered. 'That's a pretty unusual name.'

'Not in Greece.'

No way could fate be that cruel. 'He's Greek…?' she asked with extreme casualness.

Tom nodded. 'That's right. We were at Oxford University at the same time, though Nik dropped out before he graduated.'

'That doesn't sound like someone you'd know…' Katie gulped hoarsely. Dropping out equated with someone being reckless, someone who might at a push get into debt, someone who might resolve the problem by… *Stop this,* she told herself sternly, *you're getting paranoid.*

'You mean I'm a boring old stick.' Tom pouted, exploiting his boyish charm for all it was worth.

'You're not old…' Katie protested, subduing a flicker of irritation. 'Or boring,' she added hastily. 'You're solid and responsible.'

'That makes me feel a hell of a lot better,' Tom responded, his charm fading abruptly.

Conscious she had hurt his feelings, Katie tried to soothe his injured pride.

'Women don't actually want to marry exciting men,' Katie told him, believing it. 'They're too unreliable.' She stopped, unhappily aware that she was only making matters worse.

To her relief Tom recovered his humour and laughed loudly.

'No, they just want to make mad passionate love to them,' he suggested, thinking she looked especially adorable flushed and confused.

'Some women might, but not me,' Katie insisted firmly. 'Men like that are vain and shallow and only interested in looking cool,' she sneered.

Tom winced. 'You'll not share that with Nikos will you, sweetheart?'

'I shall hang on his every word like it's inscribed in stone,' she promised dutifully, willing to flatter his friend if it made Tom happy.

'You'll like him.'

Katie couldn't hide her scepticism.

'Women do,' Tom assured her authoritatively. 'Actually you're right, Nik wasn't in my circles of friends; in fact he was a bit of a loner. He used to ride around on this dirty great motor bike…'

Katie nodded. She was beginning to get the picture, and she didn't find it comforting. Someone reckless, who liked danger…her imagination had no problem at all picturing

Nikos Lakis in motor-bike leathers looking brooding and dangerous.

'I was there when he swerved to avoid a kid that ran out into the road. I didn't do much, but he got it into his head that I'd saved his life.'

Katie listened to his modest pronouncement with a tender smile. 'Which means you probably did.'

'I only did what anyone else would,' Tom insisted with a self-deprecating shrug. 'To be honest I was surprised when he kept in touch after he left. Apparently it caused some almighty family row when he dropped out, but everything's cosy now. His old man had a heart attack and major bypass surgery a couple of years ago and Nik took over the family firm…they're a Greek shipping family, though since the seventies they've diversified dramatically…They're billionaires… Are you all right?' he added, examining her waxily pale face with concern.

Katie took a deep breath and refocused on his anxious face. Relief made her feel quite light-headed. A Greek billionaire's son! She felt like laughing at her irrational fears. Let him be the biggest bore of the century; it no longer mattered.

'Fine.' She lifted her hand briefly to her forehead and felt a light sheen of moisture on her skin. 'Minor blood-sugar dip, I didn't have time for lunch today,' she admitted, making a silent vow to tell Tom the truth before the evening was out.

Tom frowned disapprovingly. 'They take advantage of you at that place.' He squeezed her shoulder. 'Never mind, not long now and you'll be able to hand in your notice.'

'Hand in my notice?' Katie echoed blankly.

Tom laughed. 'You'll be far too busy to work when you're my wife. Of course, if you want to continue with a little charity work…'

Katie could hardly believe what she was hearing—Tom

expected her to quit work when they were married! There was no way!

'You've got a bit more colour in your cheeks now,' he observed, blissfully unaware that it was hostility to her impending retirement that had produced the delicate tinge of creamy rose to her pale honey complexion. 'Come on, love, the sooner we feed you the better.'

'And your friend doesn't like being kept waiting,' Katie couldn't prevent herself from adding drily.

His friend called Nikos.

How stupid she'd been to be spooked by a name. There were most probably hundreds—no, *thousands* of men called Nikos in the world, she told herself as she followed Tom into the dining room.

This isn't happening!

'Here she is, Nikos.' Tom, oblivious to the frozen state of the young woman beside him, proudly pushed her forward. Like a marionette she responded stiffly. 'This is Katie. Didn't I tell you she was totally gorgeous and clever too? Come on, sweetheart, don't be shy...'

Shy? More like paralysed with shock and horror, not to mention being scared witless into the bargain! Oh, God, this meal looked like one she wasn't likely to forget in a hurry!

If the floor had opened up at her feet Katie would have jumped into the black hole rather than live this moment. Even at the best of times she hated it when Tom introduced her to his friends with this sort of fanfare. Maybe there were women out there who could live up to the sort of lavish build-up he gave her, but Katie knew she wasn't one of them.

The dark-suited, long-limbed figure rose with languid, almost feral grace to his feet. 'You did indeed, Tom.'

All thoughts of hallucination vanished. Katie hadn't heard it for seven years, but the deep, cultured voice was exactly as she recalled it. The bitter-chocolate tone with the merest hint of an accent made goose-bumps break out like a rash over her skin and had, she suspected, some worrying connection with her tingly feelings.

Despite her scornful dismissal, the *tingly* feelings continued to make their presence felt.

'Tom's told me so much about you I feel as though we already know each other.'

Unlike her, Tom didn't seem to notice the sinister, sardonic edge in the soft words or see the cold hostility in the other man's remarkable eyes as they roamed casually over her body, lingering longer than was polite on the exposed slopes of her breasts.

Despite the fact disbelief was ricocheting wildly around inside her head, Katie could almost admire his nerve, her own was very near to breaking-point. It wasn't just not knowing how or why he was here—*and that was bad enough!*—it was the not knowing what he was going to do or say next that really terrified her.

Their glances locked, the expression on those finely chiselled features revealed little, but as their eyes briefly touched Katie was left with the definite impression that he was enjoying every second of her discomfiture. It was that discovery that enabled her to hold it together.

Katie welcomed the fortifying flicker of anger; it was something solid and real for her to cling to. The malicious pleasure she'd seen in those dark, unfathomable depths was inexplicable to her. Admittedly buying a husband might make her deserving of the odd sneer and snigger in some ungenerous quarters, but if she'd been doing the buying he'd been bought, which hardly made his position one of superiority…not that you'd know, he looked so damned pleased with himself.

Though that smugness and self-satisfaction might have something to do with the billions he no doubt had in his bank account. *And I gave him money…* When her mind started working again she might be able to figure that one out, but right now she had to swallow a bubble of hysterical laughter; the situation was positively surreal.

'Katie, darling, this is Nikos Lakis.'

Like Tom, he was wearing a dark grey suit; unlike Tom's, it was not cut to disguise a spreading waistline. It was hard to imagine the man standing there indulging himself in the necessary excesses to result in a thickening waistline...everything about him was hard and he exuded an aura that said, 'I'm in control'. She'd not come across many men like that but those she had she hadn't warmed to. They thought the world revolved around them.

Her mind drifted back to the small, stuffy little ante-room of the register office. She recalled the tall, commanding figure so much younger than she'd been expecting who'd strode in displaying an unnerving *presence* and none of the humility she'd expected of a man desperate enough to marry for money. Knowing he'd been born with a solid gold spoon in his distressingly sexy mouth explained the arrogance, but not why a billionaire's son had married for money.

My God, I've been married to a Greek million...no, billionaire for seven years and I didn't even know it. Even the most soapy of daytime soaps wouldn't dare come up with a storyline that far-fetched.

Katie was forced to revise her opinion about control slightly as her wide, shock-glazed eyes slid to the passionate curve of his wide, sensual lips...the light, quivering sensation in her belly intensified. If he did lose control he'd probably do it in a spectacular way. A totally inappropriate mental image of those predatory lips crashing down on her own flashed across her vision...

Katie was just getting on top of her wayward imagination when her nightmare smiled—it wasn't helpful. The smile exuded a sensual menace totally in keeping with her wild imaginings. Her bemused brain sought refuge in irrelevant details like the sculpted curve of his lips and the slashing angle of his high, angular cheekbones. Over the years she'd decided that her imagination had exaggerated the raw sexuality Nikos Lakis exuded—she now knew differently! The man oozed sex appeal from every pore; it was hardly decent.

Katie's obedient lips did the necessary social smiling, but her eyes were another matter; they continued to broadcast horror, confusion and bewilderment.

Tom, cheerfully oblivious to the screaming tension or her reluctance, pulled her farther forward with pride.

'Pleased to meet you, Katherine.' One dark brow quirked. 'It is *Katherine*...?'

She glared...he knew full well it wasn't. Like herself, he had a copy of the marriage certificate that Harvey had locked safely away...*Harvey*! The trusted family friend must have known his identity and he hadn't told her—the duplicity of men was staggering, she thought, wisely skimming over her own forays in that direction of late.

'No, actually it's Katerina.' *Do you, Katerina, take...* She gave her head a little shake to chase away the intrusive memory. 'Only nobody calls me that any more,' she added, anxiety and escalating antipathy making her soft voice terse and sharp.

'That's a pity, it's a beautiful name.'

It was the way he said it, but then a bus timetable would sound dreamy when spoken by that silver tongue. No, not silver—if that deep, velvet-textured drawl had a colour it would be a deep, decadent purple. She gave her head a tiny shake, irritated by the whimsical nature of her thoughts. Purple or puce, a voice like that constituted a very dangerous ability in a male, especially one who looked like this.

If he was as shocked as she had been to discover the identity of his dinner companion he was hiding it well, which meant what? Had he known? Maybe he didn't recognise her? She ditched that possibility before it was even fully formed. Was he here because Harvey had contacted him about the divorce? Or was this one horrible, horrifying coincidence?

Questions she had aplenty, but no obvious answers surfaced in her spinning head.

Oh goodness, why didn't I tell Tom when I had the chance…? She groaned at herself. Now it was too late… he'd hate her, and who could blame him? The fact that this was only happening because she hadn't come clean made it seem as though she was being punished for her cowardice. Perhaps it was appropriate that her retribution had come in the form of a man who possessed the sinful, dangerous beauty of a dark fallen angel.

Lips compressed to keep them from trembling, she shot the tall, dark figure a covert look from under the sweep of her long lashes. What she saw in his lean face was not comforting. *Please, please don't let him say anything until I've had a chance to tell Tom myself.*

That was it! If she could explain to Tom herself…sudden hope surged through her. Maybe it wasn't too late. If she could get this Nikos creature alone and explain how things stood, she could appeal for his temporary silence until she'd had a chance. Their eyes collided; it was a fleeting collision but enough to make her forget about appealing to his better nature. She repressed a shudder—nobody with eyes like that had one!

Of all the men in the world why had she ended up married to this one?

If Nikos Lakis kept quiet about their marriage deal it would be for his own reasons, not out of consideration for her or Tom. Maybe it didn't fit in with his macho image to admit he had married for money, she speculated. Although it seemed to her that Greek men were quite pragmatic about such things. She gritted her teeth; the best she could hope for was that he'd keep silent for his own reasons.

Katie didn't know how her trembling knees managed to

support her weight as her hand was enfolded in a firm grip. Her tummy muscles cramped violently as long, lean brown fingers folded over her own. The contrast of small and large, dark and pale…once again her beleaguered brain was distracted from coping with much more urgent matters like should she beat him to the punchline and tell Tom now herself?

How would she do that exactly…? *Actually, Tom, I've met Nikos before…yes, isn't that a coincidence? I don't know him exactly, we just got married…*

The men were talking, though the words were just a discordant buzz in her ears. Katie found she was sitting but couldn't recall taking her seat. Neither could she recall how the glass found its way into her hand, but it seemed an extremely good idea to make use of it.

With a sigh she replaced the drained glass on the table and as she shook back her hair discovered both men were looking at her.

'Is that such a good idea on an empty stomach, darling?' Tom spoke lightly but his eyes were shooting furious warning messages.

Tom was desperately anxious for her to make a good impression on this man he admired. *If only all Tom had to worry about was me having one too many drinks!* The irony struck her forcibly, and she struggled to control the bubble of hysteria lodged dangerously in her dry throat. Laughing like a hyena might just draw unwanted attention…

'Katie's had a tough day at work.'

Katie's smooth brow wrinkled…again the anxiety to please in Tom's manner. Maybe this wasn't so surprising. Two things impressed Tom, money and power, and this man had both in abundance, and it showed. Tom had money, Tom had power, what he didn't have was the tall Greek's quiet, understated confidence. Confidence that came when you didn't feel the need to prove yourself to anyone.

'You work, Katerina?' The dark winged brows knitted as Nikos Lakis managed to imbue the casual enquiry with amused incredulity.

Katie's eyes narrowed as those black eyes broadcast useless ornament. It seemed as if the antipathy she felt was fully reciprocated.

'When it doesn't interfere with shopping or polishing my nails.'

Tom, who had never heard that particular tone in her soft, pleasing voice before, laughed uncomfortably as though she'd made a joke he didn't quite understand. Nikos didn't laugh; his merciless eyes continued to rake her angry face and then, much to her dismay, his long fingers curled over her left hand, which lay clenched on the table-top.

Without haste he unfurled her tapering fingers one by one. The tip of his thumb grazed the blue-veined inner aspect of her wrist as he turned her hand over, exposing the short, unpolished condition of her nails; his touch also exposed her nerve endings, which came to tingling life.

Katie would have liked to crawl out of her skin.

'Not today,' he remarked softly.

His soft voice did things almost as uncomfortable to her as the light touch. Dabbing her tongue to the tiny beads of sweat across her upper lip, she snatched her hand away.

Breathing hard through her flared nostrils, she lifted her chin. 'I'm an events organiser.' And a flipping good one too, she felt like adding to the patronising prat.

'Impressive,' he drawled, sounding anything but impressed. 'And what does an events organiser do exactly?' he added, making it sound as though as far as he was concerned it couldn't be much.

Tom, sensing the atmosphere for the first time, looked slightly uneasy. 'Katie works for a charity, but she'll be giving up work after the wedding.'

'Ah…the wedding—and when will that be?'

'I can't get Katie to set a date.'

Nikos's lazy glance turned to Katie. '*Really?* You do surprise me.'

He reminded her of some sleek cat playing with a mouse, not because he was particularly hungry, just because it was in his nature to be cruel. The more she saw of this man, the more she saw to dislike. Kate's nostrils flared as her teeth came together in a smile that was as brittle as it was brilliant.

Two could play at this, she thought grimly. If he was going to drop her in it there didn't seem any point prolonging the agony or his pleasure.

It was a dangerous tactic, but Katie felt uncharacteristically reckless, and at least this way she'd know one way or the other.

'And you, Mr Lakis—is there a *Mrs* Lakis?' she enquired sweetly. 'Or any little Lakises?'

Katie held her breath; the silence that followed her question seemed to last for ever. When her lowered gaze lifted she was surprised to see something that might have been admiration in Nikos Lakis's dark, glittering eyes.

'There is only one *Mrs* Lakis in my life, and she's my stepmother, who's very much an active force in my life.' He smiled, not in a snide, snooty, I've-just-stepped-on-something-nasty way—anything but. Katie's jaw dropped as she watched the stern lines of his proudly sculpted face soften as he produced a real, honest-to-goodness grin.

The transformation was nothing short of devastating. Katie only just stopped herself grinning fatuously back.

'So you're not married, then?' she persisted doggedly.

'If Nik had married, Katie, I think we'd have read about it.' Tom laughed. 'The media would have had a field day.'

You don't know the half of it, Katie thought, feeling a tide of guilty colour seep up her neck. She pressed a hand to her hot cheek.

She was disgusted with herself that in her desire to score points against the detestable Nikos Lakis she'd lost track of what was most important. The public humiliation and scandal of having his fiancée revealed as being secretly married to Nikos Lakis would be devastating for Tom and her primary concern had to be protecting him from any fallout.

'Marriage is inevitable if only for the procreation of…how did you put it?…little Lakises. We Greeks are a little old-fashioned about such things.'

'I'd have said cold-blooded.'

Tom began to look seriously disturbed as he laid a warning hand on her shoulder; the pressure made Katie wince. Nikos's eyes followed the other man's gesture, and the permanent line over the bridge of his masterful nose deepened fractionally.

'Shall we order?' Tom said, patting her arm before his hand fell away.

'I'm not hungry.' Katie doubted she could have eaten a scrap even if her future had depended on it, which was no more an absurd scenario than the real one—having her future and Tom's dependent upon the discretion of a man who seemed as capricious as he was overbearing.

'Greeks are not renowned for their cold-bloodedness, Katerina.'

'Oops, was that your ego I stepped on? Oh, but I'm sure they're *spectacular* lovers.' She turned the voltage of her insincere smile up by several watts before allowing it to fade away to grim contempt. 'But pardon me if I happen to think that picking out some poor girl with good child-bearing hips and the right blood lines to produce an heir is *extremely* cold-blooded.'

'Katie!'

Nikos, a smile fixed on his sensual lips, lifted his hand in a soothing gesture to still the other man's appalled protest. 'You are marrying a *romantic*, my friend,' he drawled. 'Someone to whom arranged marriages are anathema.' He scanned her face with derisive eyes. 'Am I right, Katerina?

You would never marry for *anything* but love? Certainly not for anything as base as…security.' His long forefinger seemingly accidentally brushed the diamond nestling on her finger.

His mockery, as corrosive as battery acid, made her long to wipe the smirk off his face. Her hands curled into fists on the table-top.

'In a perfect world everyone would marry for love,' she told him stiffly.

Nikos's mobile lips curled contemptuously. 'So you are a pragmatist after all, which is of course infinitely preferable to a hypocrite.'

At his soft, sibilant words the last remnants of Katie's trepidation were washed away on a violent tide of anger. It was one sneer too many. She lifted her furious sparkling eyes to his lean, dark face—just where did he get off looking down his superior nose at her?

Buying a husband might be a pretty pathetic thing to do, but at least she'd had a damned good excuse, whereas what excuse had Nikos Lakis had? A quick way to get money to fuel his extravagant lifestyle when he'd fallen out of favour with his rich daddy seemed the safest bet. *If anyone is the hypocrite here, it isn't me,* Katie thought scornfully.

Tom, who had the suspicion he was missing something in this rapid exchange, seized on the mention of something he felt he was an expert on. 'Oh, Katie is very practical.'

Nikos looked from the ring on her finger to the diamonds encircling her narrow wrist and smiled. 'That I never doubted. Ah, I hope you don't mind, I ordered champagne,' he said as a wine waiter approached the table.

'Much appreciated, Nik. Isn't it, darling?'

Katie nodded. It pained her deeply to see Tom's unsuspicious pleasure at the empty gesture. Normally an astute man, he couldn't seem to see what was under his nose where Nikos Lakis was concerned. Maybe it was the glamour of his wealth that made Tom blind. As far as she was concerned, the man was a prize creep!

Nikos took the bottle from its bed of ice and personally popped the cork with an expert twist of his long brown fingers and a flick of his strong, supple wrist, but then he would be an expert at drinking champagne and making love to beautiful women, Katie thought sourly, for wasn't that what playboys like him spent their time doing? The irony was that she had probably financed some of that champagne and those women! The realisation only made his attitude all the more hypocritically sanctimonious.

Her chin firmed in determination; they'd had a deal and he'd got his money's worth for precious little effort on his part. She was damned if she was going to let him ruin her life just when it was going where she wanted it with his silent threats, and the first moment she got him alone she was going to tell him so.

The thought of being alone with him made her stomach flip. Katie was surprised to discover that excitement and disgust could sometimes feel much the same thing. Naturally, given the choice she'd never want to be alone with the hateful man, but under the circumstances there wasn't an option.

'To the happy couple.'

Katie, her eyes shining with belligerence, obediently sipped the expensive bubbles, not tasting a thing.

The meal was torture; Nikos's cryptic remarks were so numerous that Katie was sure Tom would catch on. It took all her will-power not to react to his wind-ups. The intrusive chime of Tom's mobile just as they reached the main course was for once something of a welcome break.

He apologised but took the call and spoke for several minutes to someone on the other end. From the way his expression darkened it wasn't hard to tell it was bad news he was hearing.

'I'll be there in about thirty minutes,' he said, before

sliding his phone back into his pocket. 'I'm really sorry, folks.' His apologetic glance slid from Katie to Nikos and back again. 'But I really have to go. That out-of-town development I'm working on has been nothing but trouble from the start. I'd heard there was going to be some sort of demonstration so I arranged for the bulldozers to move in tonight, but it seems the damned eco-warriors beat us to it.

'And,' he added gloomily, 'they're not alone. A local TV station has picked up on it.' Looking grim, he folded his napkin and got to his feet. 'Can you believe it? All this over a scrubby bit of bog land nobody has ever heard of. Now they've come up with rare weed…I ask you, a *weed*!'

Katie, who found she had some sympathy with the local businesses and residents who didn't want the out-of-town development, kept a tactful silence.

'Some people,' he complained darkly, 'can't stand progress.'

'The future, my friend, is green,' Nikos observed.

Tom's laughter suggested he considered his friend's remark a joke. Katie, who wasn't so sure, began to get to her feet.

Tom motioned her to sit down. 'No, sweetheart, you finish your meal—no need for everyone to suffer. Nik will see you home?' He looked enquiringly at the other man, who responded smooth as silk.

'My pleasure.'

Katie's stomach gave a horrid lurch. Only a determination not to give him the satisfaction enabled her to conceal her dismay.

'Thanks, mate.' Tom gave Nikos a thumbs-up signal. 'You two enjoy your meal,' he encouraged, bending down to kiss the top of Katie's head.

'Perhaps I could help,' she said, speaking quickly. 'I know Mark Rogers's mother.' Tom gave a growl at the mention of the leader of the local opposition to his project.

'She's a lovely woman, Tom, and she was saying that it's the scale of the development and the lack of local consultation that has upset Mark and the others. Perhaps if—'

'I appreciate the offer, Katie,' Tom said, unable to hide his impatience. 'But this is business. I'm sure Rogers's mother is a nice woman, but you can't reason with troublemakers like him—they just see it as weakness. I'll ring you in the morning.'

Katie had told herself that that was just the way Tom was and it wasn't something she could do anything about, but on this occasion as she watched his departure part of her wanted to call him back and confront him. *Why are you acting like a prehistoric jerk? Why are you treating me like a brainless ornament?* she wanted to demand.

She'd seen him work perfectly amicably with high-powered female executives. He'd come across as an enlightened new man on the occasions she'd heard him express admiration for females in top jobs. So why, when it came to his own fiancée, did he assume that anything remotely connected with his business was over her head?

Maybe it was his upbringing, she reflected, *or maybe I just look dumb?*

She gave a sigh as he reached the door and, turning back to the table, discovered that Nikos Lakis was watching her.

CHAPTER THREE

'WHAT,' Katie snapped testily, 'are you looking at?' There was entirely too much understanding in those disturbing eyes of Nikos's for her comfort.

'The dynamics of a loving relationship.'

The reply didn't soothe her; she didn't want those cold, clever eyes dissecting her relationship with Tom.

Maybe you're afraid he'll make you see something you don't want to?

Katie turned her attention back to the food on her plate; it was hard to simulate interest in the beautifully prepared meal.

'He's going to ring you…so you've not moved in together…' Nikos regarded her down-bent head speculatively from over the rim of his glass.

'No, we haven't.'

'Shrewd and beautiful?' he drawled admiringly. 'No doubt your tactics have a lot to do with a confirmed bachelor like Tom popping the question. Living together inevitably makes a man less eager to commit to marriage.'

With unwarranted viciousness Katie speared an innocent butter-coated new potato with her fork; it made a poor substitute for what she longed to stab.

'Seeing their beloved first thing in the morning rarely matches up to a man's romantic fantasy,' he observed in a superior, amused tone.

'Like *you'd* know such a lot about romantic fantasy!'

Nikos didn't seem offended by her gibe. 'Oh, I wasn't referring to myself; you're right, I'm no romantic. I don't expect or particularly want perfection in a woman and I was seventeen the last time I put one on a pedestal. Tom on the other hand…' His arched brows rose.

Katie lifted her head from her prolonged contemplation of her food. 'Tom does not put me on a pedestal!' she retorted uneasily. 'That's a disgusting thing to say!' Her nose wrinkled with distaste at the idea.

'Disgusting…?' His broad shoulders lifted. 'An interesting choice of adjective.' His upper lip curled in a cynical sneer. 'I'd have thought that being worshipped was most women's dream.'

'Being *loved* is most women's dream.' *Oh, God, I sound like a starry-eyed teenager…* Her resolve stiffened as she stuck her chin out fully expecting his scorn—why should she be embarrassed by something that she believed? She wasn't going to let some dyed-in-the-wool cynic make her feel self-conscious. After all, you couldn't expect someone like Nikos Lakis to appreciate the difference between being loved for what you were and being loved for what someone wanted you to be.

Their eyes touched; hers were defiant, his were… Katie swallowed; then again maybe Nikos understood more than she thought. Uneasily she observed the subtle shift in his expression as he registered her loaded riposte.

Without saying anything he made her feel she'd just made some remarkably revealing comment.

'Tom *loves* me,' she gritted. 'And he doesn't care how I look in the morning. I suppose *you* look marvellous after a late night,' she snarled.

The instant the words were off her tongue Katie knew they'd been a bad idea. It was like opening the floodgates of her imagination. Unwelcome images of tousled dark hair, slumberous, sexy eyes and hard, olive-toned flesh minus any form of clothing—Nikos Lakis *definitely* slept naked—flashed through her undisciplined mind. She sucked in air through her flared nostrils and then exhaled hard through her parted lips.

Thoughtfully Nikos watched the soft colour mount the smooth contours of her cheeks. 'Actually I've not had any complaints as yet,' he revealed softly.

The colour in her cheeks deepened. 'Amazing what some women will put up with if they think they stand the chance of snagging a rich man,' she grunted contemptuously.

'I bow to your superior experience in such matters.'

It was the closest he'd come yet to an outright accusation of gold-digging. Katie's fork fell from her grasp; she barely registered the noisy clatter of the metal on porcelain.

'I wouldn't kiss a man before he's cleaned his teeth in the morning for any amount of money!' she declared loudly enough to draw the amused attention of several diners close by who heard her forthright words.

For the first time she had the impression her response had perplexed Nikos. His glance slid to the undulations of her heaving bosom before returning to her angry face.

'If you really mean that, I think you've been spending your nights with the wrong sort of man.'

Katie, her attention hopelessly held in thrall by the low, husky throb of his voice, watched as the heavy lids of his exotically slanted eyes dropped lower over his dark glittering gaze.

Elbows planted on the table, he leaned towards her, it seemed to Katie's feverish mind that his closeness had cut them off from the rest of the room. Her senses were teased by the elusive male fragrance he used and the even more elusive but naturally occurring faintly musky male scent rising off his warm skin.

'There is a special sort of pleasure in kissing someone and tasting the scent of your body on their lips...' With each successive syllable his voice dropped lower until it was just a husky purr. The mesmeric drawl sent tiny shivers trickling through her body. 'The intimacy awakens memories of the pleasures of the night before,' he rasped.

The images that filled her brain sent a scalding hot flash

of heat washing over Katie's body, sending her core temperature off the scale. Katie tore her eyes from the dark ones of her tormentor. It would have been a lot less humiliating to pretend that it hadn't happened…that Nikos Lakis *hadn't* turned her into a mindless bundle of lustful longing with a bit of coarse sexual innuendo, but he had.

Forewarned is forearmed, she told herself without any particular conviction—there were some things even she, the eternal optimist, found hard to put a positive slant on.

'Give me fluoride any day,' she gritted stubbornly.

For a moment Nikos looked nonplussed by her response. Then a slow grin spread across his lean face. Katie found her eyes drawn to the brown flesh of his throat as, head back, he laughed. Presumably his skin would be that firm and golden elsewhere?

'And you, Katerina…'

'Me…?' she squeaked, lifting a hand to cover the mortified colour in her cheeks. To be caught drooling was bad enough, but to be caught drooling over Nikos Lakis made her certifiably stupid!

'Am I wrong to think that you feel some sympathy for these little flowers that Tom is going to cover with concrete?' He leaned back in his seat and replaced his almost full wineglass on the table.

She was unable to match his mental agility; the abrupt change of subject escalated Katie's growing mental confusion.

'What?' she asked, playing for time. It was unthinkably disloyal to voice her doubts on the subject to anyone, let alone this man. 'I'm totally behind Tom.'

'Even when you think he's wrong. How loyal.'

'Tom would never do anything illegal.'

'*Legally*, I'm sure he wouldn't do anything wrong.'

All thoughts of confronting Nikos and reminding him he had to honour his side of their bargain had long since vanished from her head. Katie just knew she'd explode or do something equally socially unacceptable if she spent another moment in this detestable man's company!

'How dare you? I'm not going to sit here and debate my fiancé's morals with someone like you,' she spat in a shaking voice as she rose to her feet. The abrupt but graceful motion sent the soft fabric of her dress hissing softly around her shapely ankles.

'Not a pudding girl, then?' The lazily mocking observation was addressed to her rigid slender back. Nikos spent the next few moments until she disappeared from view admiring the elegant line of her stiff spine and the gentle sway of her softly curved behind. The image, though quite delectable, brought a brooding frown to his face.

It wasn't easy when every cell in her body was agonisingly aware of him, but Katie stubbornly refused to acknowledge the tall figure at her side as she stood in the foyer—nobody else felt similarly inhibited. She had never felt so conspicuous as she did standing next to someone that everyone seemed inclined to goggle at—so much for good old British reserve! For his part Nikos seemed genuinely oblivious to the intense interest he created.

It was only when he cancelled the request for a taxi she'd made to the uniformed figure who arrived all effusive apologies for his absence at the reception desk that Katie could no longer pretend he wasn't there.

'Go away,' she spat. 'Or I'll call Security.' Her fury was fed by the fact the receptionist was automatically obeying him despite her loud protest.

'I'm taking you home; it is what Tom would expect.'

This struck Katie as the height of hypocrisy. 'The same way he'd expect you to insult me every chance you get.' If he thought she was getting in his car with him he was off his head—*or I would be if I did,* she thought, recalling uneasily the strange things that happened to her when she was in close physical proximity to him…

Her delicate feathery brows drew together. Something as shallow and superficial as sexual attraction ought in theory to be easy to control or at least ignore…

'Is that what I've been doing?'

Katie lifted confused eyes to his. 'I don't know what you've been doing,' she revealed shakily. She bit her lower lip and added in a hard, contemptuous voice, 'I should have known you'd be the sort of man who'd drink and drive.'

Katie watched in reluctant fascination as the handsome face above her grew taut and forbidding… *My Lord, he really is formidable,* she thought, unable to tear her gaze free.

'If you were half as observant as you like to think yourself you'd have noticed that, unlike you, I barely had a mouthful of wine,' he announced austerely.

'Are you calling me drunk?' she demanded spikily.

Nikos muttered something inaudible but definitely not English or polite under his breath. 'That at least would be some excuse,' he gritted. 'But I think your unreasonable behaviour is a result of an intractable, obstinate and shrewish disposition, not inebriation.'

'I hate to disillusion you but not agreeing with you is not actually the accepted litmus test for pigheadedness. Just because women fall in with your wishes doesn't mean they actually agree with you, or even think that pearls of wisdom fall from your tongue.' Pausing to catch her breath, she delivered a breathless, snide laugh. 'It just means you've got more money than they have. Privately they probably think you're just as much of a pain as I do.'

Incredulity—maybe people didn't speak to him that way?—metamorphosed into sizzled anger in his dramatic eyes and Katie wondered with a strange sense of objectivity if she might not have gone too far. It was almost as if she had a compulsion to push him, test him to his limits.

'I can only assume,' he replied in a voice with a chill factor straight from Siberia, 'that Tom has been kept in ignorance of this charming aspect of your personality—he never struck me as a stupid man, but then I suppose a beautiful face will make the wisest man foolish,' he concluded cynically.

It wasn't the attack alone that made her eyes open wide in amazement, it was the inference that he thought she had a beautiful face... Her preoccupation with this discovery struck her as unhealthy. She'd never counted vanity as one of her sins...now pride and obstinacy were quite another matter!

'Now be a good girl and let me take you home.'

His patronising drawl fanned the embers of her temper into hot flame. 'Go jump in the lake!' she bawled childishly up at him. As she was tall, Katie wasn't accustomed to being forced to tilt her head back to look a man in the face. She silently seethed with discontent. It wasn't fair, she reflected resentfully, that simply because the gene pool had made him so damned tall he immediately had an unfair advantage in any argument...

'If you are still concerned that I have been drinking, don't be,' he continued sombrely. 'I am very conscious that cars can be a lethal weapon—my elder brother was killed by a drunk driver.'

His frosty manner was not one that invited sympathy; despite this, Katie's attitude tumbled abruptly from extreme hostility to aching pity. Notwithstanding his terse tone, she was convinced that behind that stony façade he was hurting.

She knew of course it was probable that the Peter factor had something to do with her response—up to this point they'd had nothing in common, but now she knew that they'd both lost their brothers in motor accidents. Though the circumstances were very different, she felt, quite illogically, that some tenuous link had sprung up between them—not enough to make them inseparable friends, but maybe it just made him seem a little more human, more fragile. Fragile…? She glanced up at his tough profile and shook her head; maybe that was taking it too far.

It was ironic, considering that she'd been trying to discover a weak spot in his defences all evening, that now she had actually found one all she wanted to do was kiss him better. *Kiss…don't go there, Katie.* But of course she did.

Her active imagination had rapidly progressed beyond the kissing scene; by now things had got a lot further! Katie stopped herself; she was sure Nikos Lakis was the person in the universe *least* likely to need to be kissed better.

'I'm sorry about your brother.' *I suppose I just don't have the killer instinct.*

Nikos's dark, well-defined brows drew together as he watched those extraordinary sapphire-blue eyes fill until they glistened luminously with unshed tears. It struck him as bizarre that someone so hard-nosed and single-minded should have tears to spare for someone she had never even met.

This unexpected display of empathy was totally incompatible with the character of the woman that he had in his mental file marked 'Katerina Forsythe'. Nikos scowled; he didn't want her to be more complex than the two-dimensional character he had imagined. Mostly he considered himself pretty flexible and open to new ideas, but in this instance he was extremely resistant to revision.

'And I'm sure you're an excellent driver,' she added generously. 'But I've no intention—'

His deep, strangely abstracted voice cut softly across her rambling rejection. 'I thought that day I first saw you that you were wearing tinted contact lenses, the colour of your eyes was so…*extreme*. But the colour is real, isn't it?' His expression took on an almost accusing cast as he gazed down into the clear blue of her widely spaced, darkly fringed eyes.

The total unexpectedness of his comment made her blink, or maybe the intensity of his regard had something to do with her need to break the contact? It surprised her that he'd even noticed what colour her eyes were, let alone given the shade any thought.

'Of course it's real.' For some inexplicable reason her heart began to act as if she'd decided to sprint across the lobby.

Nikos cleared his throat and ran a long-fingered hand through his dark glossy hair. 'It is a very unusual colour—almost violet. Did you inherit your colouring from your mother?'

The tight feeling in her chest made her voice sound unusually breathy when she replied. 'No, my mother was very dark. It was Peter who inherited her colouring.' Her expression softened as she thought of Eleri's glossy jet-black hair and golden skin. 'Dad was a blue-eyed, redheaded Scot.'

'*Was?* Is he dead?'

'They both are.'

'So there is just you and...Peter? Or do you have other siblings?'

Katie shook her head. 'No, it was just us two—and Peter, he died.'

'Long ago?'

'Seven years.'

He nodded, but did not comment further on what she'd told him.

Katie wasn't quite sure *why* she had told him. Peter wasn't a subject she discussed with anyone, though sometimes the weight of her secret made her long to share the burden with someone.

'I know my presence disturbs you, Katerina...'

And then some! 'Are you surprised? I wasn't expecting Tom's billionaire friend to turn out to be the penniless man I married seven years ago?'

If Nikos heard the unspoken question in her resentful

observation he chose to ignore it. Katie was starting to get the idea he did that a lot.

'If you put aside your animosity…'

Katie was unable to restrain her incredulous laughter; as if he were the soul of impartial reason! 'I don't think I'm the only person with an animosity issue here, mate.'

'If you stop spitting and snarling for a minute you might recognise that we have things to talk about.' His brows lifted to a quizzical angle. 'Don't you agree?'

Katie opened her mouth and then closed it again; she could hardly deny it. You couldn't really meet up with a man you'd just requested a divorce from and *not* talk.

'Now seems an excellent opportunity,' he continued, his eyes observing the inner struggle very clearly revealed on her expressive face.

Katie swallowed and, without looking directly at him, nodded her consent.

CHAPTER FOUR

FOR someone who'd wanted to talk, Nikos showed precious little inclination to do so once they were in his car—predictably a low-slung luxurious sports car. In Katie's present mood she'd have criticised his driving had the opportunity arisen, but it didn't. He proved to be competent but not dangerously erratic as many men were when placed behind the wheel of a powerful car.

Other than ask directions as they'd left the hotel he had said nothing at all.

She cleared her dry throat, and swallowed; it seemed it was up to her to break the ice. She wondered what to say.

'Why are you here?'

It wasn't exactly slick, but you had to start somewhere.

'When we spoke on the phone Tom could not stop talking about the woman of his dreams. I was naturally curious to see this paragon.'

Sarcastic beast. She eyed him with dislike. 'And that was it?' She gave a sceptical snort. 'I don't believe in coincidences.'

'Neither did I until I opened my mail immediately after speaking to Tom. When I read Harvey's letter relaying your request for a speedy dissolution of our union I realised why the name Katie Forsythe seemed so familiar. Katie... Katerina...I thought I'd check it out. I dropped in on Harvey on my way here and tried to get your address. Being an exemplary example of the legal profession and impervious to bribery, he refused...'

'You didn't try and bribe Harvey!' Katie exclaimed in a scandalised tone.

Nikos spared her a fleeting glance that made her feel

ridiculously gauche before he returned his attention to the narrow, ill-lit road. 'It was much simpler and more rewarding to take a look at his laptop when he was called from the office.'

This offhand attitude to such sneaky actions confirmed Katie's first impressions of his character—the man was totally without scruples. Something she would do well to keep in mind in her dealings with him.

'It might interest you to know that Harvey told me he'd personally guarantee your integrity,' she choked, regarding his perfect profile with disgust mingled with unwilling appreciation. There was a lot to appreciate: his jaw was firm without being chunky and, even though it was probably due to generations of inbreeding amongst the ruling classes, a lot of men might have sacrificed a sense of humour—you couldn't count warped—for strong features of such staggeringly perfect dimensions.

If that doesn't shame him, nothing will.

It seemed he was shameless.

'That would explain why he didn't take the most elementary security measures.' Katie looked at him blankly. 'He left the thing turned on when he left the room.'

'God knows where Harvey got the idea that you were some sort of paragon of virtue.'

'I think he received his information on my exemplary character from a prejudiced source.'

'And that would be?'

Nikos's mobile lips twitched at the corners. 'Caitlin.'

A woman, that figured, Katie thought darkly. 'What exactly did you find out when you *illegally* accessed Harvey's computer?' she interrupted uneasily.

The idea of Nikos Lakis knowing chapter and verse the intimate details of her history was not a comfortable thought.

Harvey was the only one other than herself who knew the entire story of Peter's death; the rest of the world thought, as she had until the letter written in that familiar hand had dropped on her doormat the day after his funeral, that her twin's death had been a tragic accident—a young man fond of speed who took a bend too fast on his motor cycle.

For a long time she'd just held the letter, afraid to open it and read words that seemed to come from the grave.

'Sorry, Katie,' she'd read, 'but I just can't bear the guilt.'

Katie had read on in denial, unable to think of her brother so young, so filled with life, being in such despair that he had taken his own life. *It's not possible...I would have known... I should have known...!*

'I thought I'd killed the guy, I should have stopped but I panicked and rode away. The guy lived but he's going to be paralysed for life.'

Katie had cried; she'd cried for a long time. She'd cried for her brother and she'd cried for the man whose life his recklessness had ruined.

'Why didn't you come to me?' she'd yelled at the happy, laughing face beside her own in the framed photo. 'You always come to me!' It was true the twins had always turned to one another for support in times of crisis; they'd always presented a united front against the world.

Very much later Katie had discreetly gone about finding out what she could about the man Peter had left for dead at the roadside. She'd discovered Ian Graham had been a thirty-year-old electrician. He had married his childhood sweetheart and they'd had a ten-month-old baby.

Listening in to conversations at the corner shop in the village where they'd lived had told her he had not come to terms with his disability and his young wife had been at her wits' end. Financially, the gossips had said, they'd been in a bad way; rumours had abounded that they wouldn't be able to keep up with mortgage repayments for much longer.

Katie had vowed that she'd do something to help them, even if it took her the rest of her life, which sounded very grand but the Grahams needed help now, not in twenty years' time.

It was only when she'd remembered the legacies she and Peter had been left by their Greek grandfather on condition they marry that she'd seen a way out. The shocked twins had concluded that this generosity from a grandfather they'd never even received a Christmas card from was the old man's way of controlling the grandchildren he didn't know. She and Peter had joked that they would never marry just to spite the man who through their childhood had always featured as the current villain in their games.

It was amazing really that such a strange series of circumstances had led her to exchange solemn vows with the man beside her.

'Relax, your secrets are safe, there was just your address, which revealed you shared a postcode with Tom. It therefore seemed safe to assume that my wife and Tom's angel were one and the same person.'

Katie released a gusty sigh of relief; he might be scarily perceptive but he wasn't clairvoyant. Fortunately his ability to read her thoughts—or was it her body language?—had its limitations.

'But it didn't occur to you to let me know you were coming.'

'Only momentarily,' he admitted frankly. 'But I quickly realised that your reactions might be less guarded if you had no warning.'

In other words he wanted to see me squirm and I obliged. 'Tell me,' she choked, 'did you deprive many flies of their wings when you were a little boy?'

He seemed unmoved by her withering contempt. 'Tom is my friend; I would not like to see him make an unwise marriage.'

'And marriage to me would be unwise?' Her voice rose a couple of outraged octaves, which made Nikos wince. 'You didn't seem to think so once!'

'I arrived here with an open mind.'

Katie let out a mocking howl. 'Like hell you did! What is it with you? Can't you stand to see people happy?'

'It's only natural that you would be concerned, I am going to be uncooperative about the divorce.'

Katie's eyes widened in alarm as she took an abrupt tumble from her moral high ground. 'You're not, are you?'

He didn't reply to her dismayed whisper, but his enigmatic smile seemed calculated to keep her worried. There was no point demanding a straight answer, she decided; the man seemed determined to make her squirm. He had a sadistic streak a mile wide!

'Actually when I read Harvey's letter it seemed fortuitous timing. I've been thinking of marriage myself.'

Relief flooded through Katie, who slumped back in her seat. 'That's marvellous,' she breathed happily. She supposed with his looks and money there must be any number of women out there willing and eager to overlook his overbearing and egotistical character. 'Who's the lucky girl?'

'You wouldn't know her.'

In other words, we don't move in the same circles…what a prize snob he is, she thought contemptuously.

'Why didn't you tell Tom that you were married?'

Now that was something Katie had asked herself quite a lot recently. None of the answers she'd come up with showed her in a very favourable light. 'It slipped my mind,' she responded flippantly.

He threw her a wry look.

She sighed and lifted her slender shoulders in a gesture of defeat. 'Well, I didn't *feel* married,' she told him crossly. 'And if you must know it's not an incident in my life I feel particularly proud of.'

And if she had told him, she'd have had to tell him why she'd done it, and would do again, and that wasn't an option. Nobody but Harvey knew the truth and she intended for Peter's sake it would stay that way. Her brother had paid the ultimate price for his mistake—with his life.

'I needed that money. It was a means to an end, no more, no less,' she told him coldly. 'And I had hoped that Harvey could organise things so that Tom would never have to know.'

'So your marriage is to be based on lies…excellent foundation.'

Katie flushed angrily at his sarcasm. 'I never lied to Tom. If he had asked me if I was married I would have told him.'

'So, a marriage based on half truths…I congratulate you, a *massive* improvement!'

Katie inhaled sharply. 'God, you're so sharp I'm amazed you don't cut yourself.' *I should be so lucky,* she thought viciously. 'I take it your girlfriend knows you're already married?' she added innocently.

Katie had the pleasure of seeing what appeared in the subdued light to be a faint flush highlight his high cheekbones as his jaw tightened with annoyance.

She folded her arms and smiled. 'I'll take that as a no, shall I?'

'It isn't the same thing at all.'

'Gosh!' she gasped, widening her eyes. 'That's so spooky. I must be psychic—I had the strangest feeling you were going to say that.'

His long, lean fingers tightened on the steering wheel. *'Theos!'* he thundered…the flush of anger was no longer in doubt. 'You will not speak to me in this fashion.'

'Do people always do as you say?' Katie wondered, crossing one ankle elegantly over the other.

'Yes!' he bit back.

'That must be boring.'

'Why are you marrying Tom?'

'For the usual reasons people get married.'

'You mean you're pregnant?' He shrugged as Katie gave an outraged gasp. 'So you're not pregnant.'

'Even if I was there is no shame in having a baby outside marriage.'

'My father might not agree with you there,' Nikos inserted drily as he imagined the uproar that would occur if he produced an heir but no wife. 'And,' he continued, his brows drawing together over the bridge of his nose, 'you're not in love with him. That leaves—'

'Who says I'm not in love with Tom?'

His low-pitched, mocking laugh made her prickle with antagonism.

'I can only conclude,' he added, with the air of someone who had cut through the crap and was adding two and two, 'that your nest egg has run out? Mind you, if you have many designer outfits like that one, it's hardly surprising,' he observed, allowing his eyes to briefly skim the silky blue dress and the pleasing contours it covered. 'It is a CJ Malone, isn't it?' Caitlin, he reflected, would have appreciated seeing one of her creations worn by someone who possessed the sort of unlikely proportions designers had in mind when they created outfits.

'Probably.' Katie, who wouldn't have recognised a CJ Malone if she fell over it, replied vaguely. She wasn't about to admit to him that she was wearing a hand-me-down.

'I know a lot of women with expensive tastes, but none of them who wouldn't know if they were wearing a CJ Malone.'

She shrugged. 'I'm bad on names.'

'But good at signing cheques. I suppose once you've married for money once it's easier the second time?' he mused, slowing at an unsigned crossroads.

'Left,' she replied tersely. 'You're pretty handy with the lofty disdain for someone who married for money himself, but then I suppose arranged marriages are in your blood.'

Katie was pleased to see his taut jaw tighten, presumably with anger—she *hoped* with anger. She wasn't quite sure why she wanted to make him angry and, anyway, it was hard to be sure from this angle if she'd succeeded, because his eyes were screened by the sweep of his luxuriant lashes, which cast a shadow across the high plane of his cheekbones. He had the sort of face that was aesthetically pleasing from any angle.

She arranged her own features in an expression of mock sympathy. 'What's wrong, Nikos? Did the idea of getting your hands dirty like the rest of us seem too sordid when Daddy withdrew his support?'

He slid her a look of smouldering dislike before taking the road she had indicated. 'I'm not about to explain myself to you.'

'Ditto,' she added nastily. Of all the men in the world for Harvey to produce for her to marry, why, oh, why had it been this one? Sometimes fate had a very poor sense of humour.

'Theos!' he ejaculated raggedly. 'You are the most poisonous female I've ever had the misfortune to encounter!' he gritted. 'It will be well worth the inconvenience to myself to prevent you ruining my friend's life.'

Katie stiffened as an icy shiver slid up her spine. 'What do you mean by that?'

'I think you know exactly what I mean.'

'Pretend just for a moment that I'm not a mind-reader.' She was unable to conceal the fearful quiver in her voice.

'If I thought for one moment you would make Tom happy I would give you this divorce.'

'I will make Tom happy. I love him...' she declared loudly.

A scornful sound vibrated in Nikos's brown throat. 'I watched you together; you do not love Tom,' he announced calmly.

'And you'd know, I suppose?'

'I know how a woman in love acts, and you were not that woman. There was no passion in your eyes when they touched his; you act as if he's your brother,' he sneered scornfully.

'We don't all wear our hearts on our sleeves and there is a lot more to marriage than sex!'

'Both these things are true and I agree that many successful marriages are based on more pragmatic reasons; I have no problem with that, so long as both parties enter into the arrangement with their eyes open.'

'Like us.'

'Unless you are planning on not sharing Tom's bed there are some very obvious differences, but, yes, on your part there are very obviously similarities. However, unlike Tom, I was not madly in love with you,' he ground out sarcastically. 'It is your hypocrisy in pretending you are marrying for some pure and elevated reasons that I despise. The thing you *love* is the idea of being married to someone who can buy you diamonds and keep you in your expensive clothes.'

'How dare you act as if you know me? You may have married me, but you don't know me at all!'

'But we are married and, while we are, Tom is safe from making the worst mistake of his life…'

'And you can't marry your girlfriend.' Surely that consideration had to carry weight with him.

'She will wait.' His faintly startled tone suggested no other possibility had even occurred to him.

For a brief moment Katie allowed herself the indulgence of imagining Nikos Lakis left at the altar, a shattered man. The bride leaving him in this happy vision bore a startling resemblance to herself. As pleasant as this fantasy was, Katie had to think of some way of dealing with Nikos in the real world, and denying him her favours was hardly going to do it…what would?

It was so obvious she didn't know why she hadn't thought of it earlier.

'So maybe you've got a girlfriend who will let you walk over her and wait for you until doomsday, but the press are a different kettle of fish—they don't have so much tolerance for rich playboys.'

Katie sensed his big body tense behind the wheel. *'Meaning…?'*

Katie refused to be put off by the menace in his silky voice. '*Meaning* that some sections of the press would have a field day if they found out a member of the Lakis family had gone through a fake wedding ceremony so he could get the money to maintain his lavish lifestyle.'

Greek billionaire, young and more beautiful than any man had a right to be… Katie didn't know much about such things, but she was betting the press would have files several feet thick on Nikos Lakis and more than a passing interest in his wedding plans past, present or future! Of course she would never actually go to the press, but he didn't have to know that. On this occasion, him thinking she were some avaricious cow definitely worked in her favour. She flickered a cautious glance at his profile…and swallowed; she had *definitely* made her point.

'I can just see the headlines now…' she breathed airily. Even though she was staring fixedly out the window she was aware of the explosive tension in the tall figure beside her. The silence between them lengthened until Katie could no longer bear it; she swivelled in her seat and shot a look at him.

If Nikos's expression was any indication, he was seeing those headlines she'd spoken of too. Katie salved her troubled conscience by reminding herself she would not have had to resort to these sort of tactics if he hadn't played dirty first.

'You are threatening me?' he finally asked incredulously.

Kate found his silky shark's smile and soft voice a million times more menacing than a lot of shouting and swearing.

In fact it was so unnerving that had she had any alternative or been any less stubborn she might have retracted there and then.

'Think very carefully before you do that, *yineka mou.*'

Now who was threatening…? 'I am not your *yineka mou,*' she gritted automatically, before adding, 'it's the third house on the left after the telephone kiosk.' She took some comfort from the fact that the street lights in this tree-lined avenue of solid Edwardian houses were fairly bright, and even in subdued light the car Nikos drove was likely to be noticed. He struck her as the practical type of man who would wait until there weren't any witnesses before he strangled her.

The fact that he wanted to strangle her was not in doubt!

'You speak Greek?' Nikos sounded startled.

Katie froze; her response to his sarcastic endearment had been unconscious. 'Just a few words,' she mumbled, thinking of the lullaby her mother had sung to her when she'd been unable to sleep. That and a few endearments were the limit of her vocabulary, though she wished right now that she had a better grasp of her mother tongue.

'When I visit a country,' she told him blandly, 'I make it a rule to know how to ask directions to the loo, order a drink and understand what a man is saying when he makes love to me.'

That's me, the sophisticated woman of the world, well travelled and even more well versed in other things. My God, would he laugh if he knew how far from the truth this was; the only time her passport had come out of mothballs was on a day trip to Calais and as for the other! There could be few twenty-five-year-olds less experienced!

All regretful thoughts of bilingualism and the blank page that was her sex life left her head as they rounded the next tight corner.

'Oh, my goodness…! Stop the car!' she suddenly shrieked urgently.

'There is no need for theatrics, or threats. Be reasonable.

I would be a bad enemy to make and a resourceful woman like you will no doubt find another gullible man with a fat bank balance. But I cannot permit you to marry Tom.'

Katie wasn't listening to these powerful words as she literally bounced in her seat in frustration. 'I said stop the car!' she bellowed, grabbing the steering wheel.

There was a short-lived tussle during which the car slewed violently to the left, barely missing a large beech tree before Nikos, white-faced and cursing, brought the vehicle safely to standstill.

'Are you mad?' he thundered, raking her face with silver-shot blazing eyes. 'You could have killed us.'

Katie, who had been thrown against the door, shook her head to clear the ringing in her ears. 'Well, if you'd done what I said instead of ignoring me…' she retorted, reaching for the door handle.

Long brown fingers came to cover her own.

'You are not going anywhere…'

Katie turned her head impatiently towards him. 'Shut up and phone for the fire brigade—that's my flat over there with smoke pouring out of the damned window.'

'Theos!'

CHAPTER FIVE

KATIE didn't wait around to see if Nikos was doing as she requested. She tore open the door, which he no longer barred, and, gathering her long skirts, ran full pelt down the path to the entrance she shared with Sadie.

In between pounding on the door she fumbled in her purse for her key. Before she found it Sadie, dressed in a baggy pair of silk trousers and a low-cut top that made her look like an inmate of a harem, appeared blinking sleepily.

'Where's the fire...?'

Katie had no time to waste on explanations. 'Upstairs.'

Sadie's eyes widened as she appreciated for the first time the urgency in Katie's manner. 'You're serious!' She sniffed the air. 'I can smell smoke.'

Katie barged unceremoniously past her friend. 'That's because my flat's on fire, and Alexander is still in there!' she yelled over her shoulder as she raced up the stairs two at a time.

She ignored Sadie's alarmed cry of 'Katie, you can't go up there...he's just a cat!'

The smell of smoke got stronger as she climbed the stairs, but when she arrived at the top all she could see that was out of the ordinary were a few puffs of pale smoke oozing from the gap under the door of her attic apartment—it wasn't good, but Katie had expected worse. With any luck the fire brigade would arrive before it got out of hand.

For a moment she stood there indecisively, at a loss to know what to do next. What did people do under such circumstances...?

'If in doubt cross your fingers,' she declared unscientifically. Taking a deep breath, she opened the door.

She exhaled noisily with relief as no lethal fireball knocked her over, and she pressed a hand flat against her chest where her thudding heart was trying hard to escape.

Perhaps this is my lucky day after all… she mused. *'Lucky…!'* She rolled her eyes. *Oh my word, I'm turning into one of those irritating people who see a bright side to a calamity, no matter how dire.* 'There's optimism, Katie, and then there's insanity. Your flat is on fire because you forgot to turn off your iron—that's not lucky, it's disastrous.'

The sound of her own voice calmed her nerves and strengthened her resolve. Her flat consisted of an open-plan living-area-cum-kitchen and a small bedroom with *en suite* facilities. Though the main room was filled with an acrid smoke that stung the back of her throat and made her eyes water, Katie could see no more obvious signs of the fire, which seemed to advance her theory that it had started in the bedroom. That was where she had ironed the creases from her dress on the floor rather than be bothered getting out her ironing-board.

'Alex…good puss, nice kitty,' she called, advancing cautiously into the smoke-filled room.

She had barely gone a couple of yards into the room when the visibility became nil. The only thing she could now see was a dull orange coming from underneath her bedroom door; it was the only thing that gave her any sense of orientation in the gloom. It also gave her a deep sense of foreboding…how long would the door contain the flames?

At times like this a well-developed imagination was not helpful.

No good thinking about that, she told herself, *just get on with it. The sooner you find that damned cat, the sooner you can get out.* Despite this stoicism her knees were shaking as she cautiously proceeded.

She stopped every few feet to listen but there was no response to her calls.

Katie didn't know why she had expected him to respond, because Alexander was not a nice kitty, or a good puss, he was a belligerent animal who brought live mice into her bedroom and spat when you tried to show him affection. If he'd been human, doctors would have said he had a personality disorder.

And if I had any sense, she reflected grimly, I'd leave him to fry!

'Alex, puss, puss...' Mid coaxing call she walked straight into a solid object—the coffee-table she'd discovered in the garage sale. The impact of solid teak on her vulnerable shin was enough to send her to her knees. She eased her weight from her bruised knee and felt the tangled fabric of her dress rip.

'Damn!'

It was while she was on her knees that she realised the smoke was thinner nearer the floor. She decided to continue her search from this position.

She was crawling cautiously along when she heard a deep voice calling her name.

Nikos...well, if he wants to murder me this would be the ideal opportunity, she thought. If ever there was a situation where black humour was appropriate, this was it, she decided, continuing her search, studiously ignoring his increasingly urgent cries.

Her grim smile turned into a cough when she heard a loud sound of impact closely followed by a strong Greek curse. It must, she realised in retrospect, have been the cough that alerted him to her position because moments later she was aware of strong hands sliding underneath her arms and hoisting her off the ground.

'Let me go, you fool!'

'Be still and keep calm. I have you.' He did, in an iron

grip that made escape impossible. 'You are quite safe now,' a deep, soothing voice in her ear informed her.

Katie, who had no desire to be saved, knew instinctively that *safety* was something Nikos Lakis's arms would never offer her. It was the thought of what they might offer that made her start to struggle in earnest. As several of her blows connected the reassuring note in his deep voice began to sound a lot more strained.

She let out a shriek as he stopped trying to gently soothe her when, reverting to character, without so much as a 'by your leave' he threw her resistant body over his shoulder fireman-fashion.

This is a classic case, she told herself, lapsing into exhausted passivity, *of resistance being quite definitely futile.*

Katie was forced to maintain this undignified position until they had reached the hallway when she found herself plonked on the wooden floor, which Sadie had only had stripped and polished before Christmas… *Oh, God, poor Sadie…! And this is all my stupid fault! I'm the tenant from hell!*

She felt cool fingers press against the pulse point at the base of her throat, then a hand, the same one presumably, slid under her chin and began to firmly tilt her head back.

Her watering eyes shot open; embarrassingly it seemed that Nikos had wrongly attributed her sudden inertia to a loss of consciousness. She was ashamed that for a spilt second she had actually considered letting him try to revive her—her curiosity was purely of the scientific variety, of course.

'Will you stop that?' In her head her voice had been strong and defiant, but annoyingly what actually emerged from her dry lips was a weak croak.

'Well, that's a relief, you don't require mouth to mouth,' said the big figure who was straddled over her body as he settled back on his heels.

Though his face and clothes were blackened and soot-stained, he still managed to looked as incredibly handsome as ever, Katie noted despairingly.

'Imagine your relief and quadruple it,' she croaked.

'I did not expect gratitude for saving your life, but civility would have been nice...'

'Saving my life!' she squeaked, struggling to sit up. 'My life didn't need saving, I had everything under control until you got all Neanderthal.' Panting and unable to rise, she grabbed onto the first available solid support to provide leverage, which happened to be his thighs, which were clamped either side of her waist.

The iron-hard firmness she encountered made her pause and caused her sensitive stomach muscles to tighten; escape somehow seemed less urgent as her splayed fingers explored a wider area and discovered no give in the bulging contours.

Then she came to herself and was deeply ashamed. It was unforgivable under the circumstances that she'd wasted precious seconds.

'Thanks to you,' she snarled, 'Alexander is probably frying in there,' she informed him, sliding out from between his legs and struggling to her feet. She got to them when, unaccountably, her knees gave way.

Nikos, a startled expression on his face, had also got to his feet, but with considerably more agility and athletic grace than she had. He caught her as she slid to the floor, which cushioned the impact of her contact with the bare wood.

With her head thrust between her knees, Katie batted blindly with her hands connecting only with empty air. It was only after she stopped fighting that he let her up.

'You stupid, *stupid* man!' she quavered, wiping with the back of her hand angry tears that coursed down her filthy face leaving paler tracks in the grime. Nikos, who was kneeling beside her, did not look particularly chastened by her attack. 'Alexander is still in there.' She gestured towards the door.

Nikos looked grim. 'I heard you. Stay calm—hysteria will achieve nothing.'

'I am calm!' she bellowed.

'Why on earth didn't you tell me what you were doing earlier? Surely this was not the time to preserve your image?'

Katie's brow creased in impatient bewilderment—image, what image? As for staying calm, the part of his recrimination she did understand was not only unjust, but would, if she'd been the type given to throwing wobblers, have set her off again. Katie was rendered speechless—but only temporarily.

'Like you gave me a chance!' she yelled. Or would have yelled if she hadn't been coughing so much.

'Katie…oh, Katie! You're all right, thank goodness!' A sobbing Sadie gasped as she reached the top of the staircase. 'Oh, my, I really should lose a couple of pounds,' she moaned, clutching her chest. 'I'm signing into that fat farm next week…'

Nikos was looking with some bewilderment at Sadie, who was babbling wildly on about the detox therapies guaranteed to shed the pounds.

It seemed likely to Katie he was about to make one of his nasty sarky remarks.

Katie elbowed him hard, wanting to protect her friend from his nasty tongue. 'She's terrified, it's her way of coping,' she hissed at him. God, the man had the empathy of a brick.

Nikos seemed to take her explanation on board. Nodding, he left her side with a terse instruction to *stay put*!

'Just take some deep breaths.' Katie watched in astonishment as, with a smile of incredible charm and gentle manner, Nikos bent over Sadie.

The sound of Nikos's voice seemed to calm Sadie, who

nodded and looked up at him gratefully. Katie saw her do a double take and then an appreciative grin spread over her face.

'Are you asthmatic?' Nikos asked.

'No, just fat and unfit.' Sadie laughed shakily. 'I ran all the way from the gate,' she explained. 'I think the fire brigade are coming. I heard them in the distance. Shall I go back and wait for them…?'

'Take Katerina downstairs, and leave the house immediately.'

I suppose, Katie thought numbly, *that people like Nikos come into their own in situations like this—situations that require someone to take charge and make decisions. Not even his worst enemy—which might be me—can accuse Nikos of having a problem with decision-making,* she conceded wryly.

'I'm not going anywhere until Alexander—'

'I will get Alexander and you will leave the building,' Nikos announced in a lordly fashion. 'How old is he?' he asked, advancing towards the door from which smoke was now billowing.

'You can't go in there,' Katie said positively, as convenient as it might be, she couldn't let the rat die for her cat, who might still have a few of his lives left.

'Concentrate.'

Katie was, on the amazing silver flecks in his eyes. She was stressed, exhausted, terrified, and frankly there couldn't be a worse time to admit that you were sexually attracted to a person, and had there been any other conceivable explanation for the way her mind disintegrated and her body came to life around him Katie would have plumped for it.

'How old is he?' Nikos asked as though she hadn't spoken.

The relevance of this escaped Katie, but she recognised she wasn't totally immune to the indefinable something

Nikos possessed that inspired compliance, no matter how silly the question or request.

'Threeish, I think.' That was what the vet had estimated when he'd given the ginger tom his injections. 'I think we'll sedate him next time,' he'd said drily as he'd disinfected the scratches on his arm.

Nikos stopped in his tracks. *'Three!'* he ejaculated, his lips twisting in a grimace of appalled disgust. His chest lifted. 'You left a three-year-old child alone?'

Katie's jaw dropped. He thought…he actually thought she…! Words failed her. God, she'd known he had a low opinion of her, but she hadn't thought it was *this* low!

Sadie, who was supporting Katie, came to her aid. *'Child?'* She looked at the tall Greek as though he'd gone mad. 'Alexander is a cat.'

At her words Nikos, whose body was primed for action, each muscle clenched in anticipation of the task ahead, went quite still. Only his eyes moved; they slid from Katie to Sadie, who nodded, before returning to the original object of his scrutiny.

Katie observed the muscles in his throat move as he swallowed.

'You risked your life for a cat?' There was no discernible inflection in his voice.

'Sorry, I realise it would have suited you much better if I had left a helpless baby alone.'

He gave an impatient frown. 'What are you talking about, suited *my* purposes? I have no hidden agenda.'

'You're right—it's not hidden, it's blatantly obvious. It's so much easier for you to carry on pretending you're doing the dirty to save your friend from making a terrible marriage if I reveal myself to be an avaricious monster with no redeeming characteristics whatsoever. If, however, I turn out *not* to be a heartless bitch you'll look less like the true friend and more like a spiteful, vindictive pig who can't bear to see anyone else happy because he's too emotionally retarded and shallow to form a decent relationship himself!' she concluded breathlessly.

The blank incredulity of his expression gradually metamorphosed into one of smouldering fury. 'Have you *quite* finished?' he enquired with clipped hauteur.

'Actually, no, I haven't,' Katie heard herself grit back belligerently, even though she'd run out of emotional steam.

As the expectant silence lengthened Nikos lifted a satirical eyebrow.

'I didn't risk my life. You said I did,' she reminded him. 'But I didn't,' she ended lamely. Though actually, now that she came to think about it, her actions looked a little different. This no doubt had something to do with the fact she was viewing it without the stimulation provided by gallons of adrenalin pumping through her veins.

'I might have known you wouldn't like animals,' she heard herself grouch pettishly. *Why can't I keep my mouth shut while I'm still ahead?* she wondered in exasperation. What was it about this man that made her say stupid things? When he was around she seemed to be possessed by a need to prove she was even more selfish and superficial than he thought her.

'I like animals—in fact I frequently prefer them to people, especially the crazy, stupid, female type of person.'

Katie, who was normally capable of giving as good as she got, was deeply embarrassed to feel her eyes suddenly fill with tears at this fairly mild—by his standards—insult.

She wasn't the only one to feel uncomfortable. It seemed that quite by accident she'd discovered another of Nikos's weak spots…he looked even more dismayed by her tears than she was.

He cleared his throat. 'I didn't mean…' As he spoke he seemed to notice for the first time the hand he had extended towards her. For a split second he stared at it as if it didn't belong to him, an expression of shock on his dark, lean features. Then his expression became as unrevealing as ever as he lowered it to his side. His chest lifted as he took a deep breath.

'Take Katerina outside and wait for the fire brigade,' he instructed tersely as he turned to Sadie, who silently handed him a torch from her pocket. 'Thank you.'

'I don't need taking anywhere…' Katie's voice rose to a querulous squeak as her comments fell on deaf ears. 'And you can't go back in there.'

'Look on the bright side—if I don't come out you'll be able to marry Tom.'

Katie gave a cry of alarm as he turned and stepped back into her smoke-filled flat. If it hadn't been for Sadie's restraining grip on her arm she would have followed him.

'Don't worry, he's not daft,' Sadie soothed. 'He was only trying to wind you up.' Curiously she searched her friend's face. 'He won't take any silly risks.'

This confidence from someone who had only just met the man seemed wildly misplaced to Katie. 'I am not worried, well, no more than I would be about anyone else. Absolutely not at all,' she said half to herself. 'I just can't believe he had the cheek to accuse me of risking my life. What's he trying to prove?'

'Do you mind if we discuss this outside?' Sadie wondered nervously.

'What? Yes, of course.' With one last look at the door of her flat, which Nikos had closed behind himself, Katie followed her friend down the stairs.

'What did he mean when he said—?'

'I thought you said you heard the fire brigade…' Katie interrupted, craning her head to look up the road for any sign of flashing lights.

'I thought I did,' Sadie replied apologetically.

'When that guy—?'

'Nikos,' Katie supplied distractedly.

'When Nikos said. Good grief...*Nikos*...?' You could almost hear the sound of Sadie's chin hitting her chest as the name clicked. 'You mean he's the one you...'

'I married, yes. I don't know how you can think about that when your house is on fire and it's all my fault. You should be screaming abuse at me.'

'I will if it will make you feel better, but first tell me about that *incredible* man.'

'There's nothing to tell.' Nikos was the one subject Katie wanted to avoid. Although the way things were going it didn't seem likely she would have much choice. Her choices were narrowing in other areas too. Her hopes of concealing the marriage from Tom now seemed hopelessly optimistic. She found that she was no longer thinking in terms of *if*, but *when* her sordid secret would be revealed.

'He turned up tonight—apparently he and Tom went to university together.'

'I don't believe it!' Sadie gasped, clearly startled by Katie's taut explanation. 'What were the odds on that? That must have been a bit awkward for you.'

'Ever so slightly,' Katie agreed drily.

'Has he spilled the dirt to Tom?'

'Not yet, but it's only a matter of time.' For the hundredth time in the past two minutes she glanced tensely over her shoulder towards the house. 'Shouldn't he be out by now?'

'It's only been a couple of minutes, Katie,' Sadie soothed. 'You know, I don't know how much you paid for him, but if it had been common knowledge he was available on the open market I'm betting the price would have been higher,' she joked with a lascivious grin.

'I did not buy him!' Katie denied hotly. 'Well, not like that, it was a business arrangement, nothing more.'

Sadie shrugged pacifically. 'If you say so. Are you sure you two haven't met since the wedding?'

'I don't think I'd have forgotten.' No, an encounter with

Nikos Lakis was something that stayed in a person's memory for ever like…like…eating bad shellfish, she thought sourly.

'Fair enough. It's just that you two don't talk or act like people who have as good as just met…'

Katie never had to respond to this thought-provoking observation because at that exact moment they both heard the unmistakable and very welcome shriek of a siren.

Hands folded against her chest, Katie began to jump up and down. 'They're here!' she yelled, silent tears slipping silently down her face.

Both women watched with relief as the engine drew up outside the house, disgorging several capable-looking uniformed figures. The noise of their arrival had attracted the attention of several neighbours in the tree-lined avenue, who came outdoors to investigate the activity in the normally sedate neighbourhood.

'Have I ever told you about my fireman fantasy?' Sadie caught the tail-end of Katie's incredulous expression and looked sheepish. 'Well, you have Nikos—you can hardly begrudge me a fireman.'

'He's not *my* Nikos,' Katie retorted.

'If you say so, but be a sport, Katie, I'm trying to distract myself and that one—' she pointed '—is absolutely gorgeous…'

Katie was no longer listening; she was busy running towards the fireman who had inspired Sadie's lustful fantasy.

She caught his arm and tried to speak; considering the urgency of the occasion, this seemed a bad time to lose her voice. The fire-fighter, who was probably used to dealing with people gibbering with fear, exuded a calm aura that helped Katie finally get her words out.

'Th-there's a man still in there,' she told him beckoning towards the window on the top floor.

'Has he been in there long?'

Katie swallowed and pulled distractedly at her long hair.

The sooty smell that came from it made her nose wrinkle—no doubt the rest of her smelt just as terrible and as for how she looked… *Aah, how shallow am I, thinking about my lipstick when all this is going on?* 'I don't know…it seems like a long time.' Her lips trembled and she scrubbed at her dirty face. 'It's my fault,' she confessed. 'I think I left my iron on…I knew I'd forgotten something, and now I've killed N…Nikos and Alexander.'

'There's more than one person?' he queried sharply.

'Alexander is a cat,' Sadie explained for the second time. 'Katie, he'll be fine. He didn't look like an easy man to kill to me.' Sadie smiled at the fire-fighter. 'I'm the owner, officer.'

'Hello. Is there any means of access other than the stairs?'

'There is a fire escape around the side of the house.'

Katie, not placated, shrugged off the comforting arm that slid around her shoulders. 'I'm a selfish cow, I sent him back in there for a…' Her lips began to tremble as she fearfully contemplated the consequences of her actions.

Before she could reveal to the fireman what Nikos had gone back in for there was an almighty deafening explosion as her bedroom window exploded. The fireman, his arms outstretched, shielded the two women as glass from above showered on the garden below.

'It would be better, ladies, if you waited a little farther back until the ambulance arrives.'

Katie saw his mouth move, she heard the words, but she felt as though she were in a black hole; she felt numb.

Sadie nodded, getting a firmer grip on the box containing family photos and treasures that she had automatically snatched up before they'd left the house. She urged Katie backwards while the burly fire-fighter, shouting instructions to his crew, strode off purposefully.

Katie resisted and Sadie looked with concern as the slim figure who was standing gazing with horror-filled eyes at the wicked tongues of orange flames shooting out of the window pushed her away.

'Come on, Katie, we should get out of their way,' Sadie suggested gently. 'Mrs James next door has put the kettle on.'

Katie, her arms wrapped tightly about herself, continued to rock back and forth. Under the layer of grime her skin was paper-white. 'He's dead, isn't he? I mean, if he was in there he has to be, doesn't he? Nobody could survive that.'

Sadie shrugged helplessly. 'I really don't know.' The muffled keening sound that suddenly emerged from Katie's bloodless lips before she choked it back made the hairs on the back of Sadie's neck stand on end.

The next sequence of events occurred with such bewildering speed that Sadie didn't have a chance to do anything but yell a warning to the fire-fighters as her friend, running as if all the fiends of hell were at her heels, suddenly began to pelt towards the door of the house.

Katie was never going to make it there, the two fire-fighters aiming to cut her off were closing fast, but before they had an opportunity to do so she tripped and fell. Though she landed on her knees it was the sharp pain that shot through her ankle as it turned awkwardly that made her cry out.

Just what I need—a sprained ankle, or, the way this day is going, it will probably be broken!

Impatiently brushing the tears of self-pity and impatience from her face, Katie squared her shoulders and, catching her soft lower lip between her teeth, concentrated her efforts on getting to her feet.

So far, so good, she thought as she tentatively took a cautious step; to her relief her ankle hurt but it took her weight. Wincing, she hobbled over to a convenient Japanese flowering cherry tree that was shedding its sweet-smelling blossoms onto the damp grass below and leaned against the trunk.

She gazed towards the house. The fire crew, seeing she was not seriously hurt and no longer capable of dashing headlong into a burning building, had turned their attention elsewhere.

Katie was pondering the compulsion that had been responsible for her stunt—*as if I could do something the firefighters couldn't*—when she finally recognised what the fire crew had turned their attention to. A tall figure was emerging from the smoke.

'Thank God!'

She watched through a teary haze of relief as a couple of paramedics headed purposefully towards Nikos. The incredible noise of a fire scene seemed to recede to a low background buzz and the hurrying figures appeared to slow; only her heart continued to beat fast, so fast she could feel the vibration of each inhalation in her throat. She lifted a hand to her spinning head; each breath she took was an effort.

If I faint now he'll probably accuse me of faking it to steal his moment of triumph. Only she didn't faint, the nervous tension found a more prosaic release.

'I think I'm going to be sick,' she gulped to nobody in particular, before she quietly did just that—not that anyone noticed; they were all crowding around Nikos.

Trust him to turn out to be a hero…it was a part he was born to play, she thought, a wry but relieved smile on her face as she leaned back against the tree trunk.

CHAPTER SIX

THE hero was clearly not comfortable with his moment of fame.

'I am fine.' The cough that followed this impatient pronouncement did not add weight to his claim. Ignoring a recommendation to breathe deeply, Nikos pushed aside the oxygen mask that someone was trying to slip over his head. 'I don't need that!'

'You've inhaled a lot of smoke,' the paramedic explained patiently.

Nikos smiled thinly and resisted the impulse to point out to this well-meaning individual that as the one who'd done the inhaling he didn't need any reminders. After a few moments of fruitless arguing they reached a compromise, of sorts.

'Though it is an unnecessary precaution I will come with you if you give me a few moments to speak to my wife.' Nikos gestured towards the solitary figure on the lawn and immediately regretted it because by no stretch of the imagination did she look in need of comfort. In fact she looked extraordinarily composed. 'I think she's in shock,' he improvised.

Hopefully this would adequately explain away the fact that his *wife* had been able to contain her joy at his miraculous escape. His lips curled in a cynical smile, then he shrugged; at least she wasn't a hypocrite.

'Well, just a few minutes…'

Everyone, Nikos reflected, was a sucker for a couple in love.

Did the professionals think it strange his wife had not been part of his reception committee? That she hadn't dashed to throw her arms about his neck, tears of joy running down her cheeks? Nikos did not ponder the question for long; he rarely worried about how his actions were viewed by strangers. Though the potent image did remain in his mind, not because he was thinking about the impact on others—no, it was the impact on himself that occupied his thoughts.

Smooth arms wrapped around his neck, a soft, pliant body pressed to his, a silky head close to his heart. As he closed the distance between them anyone noticing would have wrongly assumed that the dark bands of colour highlighting the slashing curve of his high cheekbones were a product of the inferno he had just escaped—they'd have been wrong.

This scenario in his head was not a displeasing one, so the primitive response of his body was not, Nikos reasoned, to be wondered at. It was an explanation he was content with, but his reluctance to release this image was less easily rationalised.

Katie levered her back from the tree trunk and pushed a large hank of heavy hair from her face. 'You found me, then…'

Nikos nodded. Her question made him realise that even though she had made no push to attract his attention, some inner radar had located her the moment he'd emerged from the building.

If you ignored the dark film of grime covering his skin and clothes he looked quite remarkably unscathed by his recent brush with death. In fact, he radiated an almost indecent amount of edgy vitality. It occurred to Katie that this was probably the most natural and relaxed she'd seen him. Near-death experiences obviously did for him what a box of chocolates, a soppy romance and a glass of wine did for her.

One corner of his mouth lifted as their eyes touched. Katie felt a flare of indignation—it clearly hadn't even occurred to him that she had been through hell and back during the last few minutes because of his ridiculous macho stunt.

She didn't know if she wanted to hit him or kiss him. Not *literally* kiss him, of course, because that would involve…her stomach took a sharp dive and the flow of her thoughts skidded to an abrupt halt. Her wide eyes were drawn by an invisible but irresistible force to the sensual curve of Nikos's mouth.

She swallowed convulsively, unable to prevent the image forming in her head of that sexy mouth claiming her own, parting her lips, his tongue invading her mouth, tasting…touching.

She shook her head and took a deep, tremulous breath. But it was too late, the chain reaction had already started.

Her eyelids fluttered as a rush of fluid warmth worked its way up swiftly from her shaking knees until her entire body was bathed in the golden glow. She held her breath and willed the flames consuming her to subside.

Katie couldn't deny she had wanted to experience that kiss for real; for several moments she had been consumed by the wanting. Even now her bones ached with the raw desire that had swept through her with the ruthless force of a forest fire.

She was guiltily aware that she had never felt that way anticipating Tom's kiss. She struggled to understand what had happened and more importantly why it was happening. It had to be her hormones; this was some sort of revenge attack because she'd neglected them.

Or maybe this wasn't just hormones—it was conceivable that she was actually suffering from some post-traumatic thing? Her flashbacks just happened to be of something that hadn't happened yet—*yet*! A grammatical error, nothing more, and she for one hated people who banged on about Freudian slips.

The more she considered it, the more she became convinced that the extraordinary things she *was* feeling were a result of the near-death thing. That sort of 'we could have died but didn't, let's go to bed' thing—it apparently happened in war situations all of the time. Her eyes widened in alarm as she realized she'd jumped from kissing to bed!

That was an alarming leap by anyone's standards.

She realised that Nikos was waiting for her to say something.

'You're not dead,' she heard herself blurt out stupidly. Stupid it might be, but it was a far safer option than begging him to kiss her.

'Sorry. I'm a bit singed if that's any help.'

Katie took a deep offended breath. 'Don't be facetious!'

Nikos inclined his head in meek acknowledgement of her censure. 'It's true, look at my eyelashes.'

'I don't want to look at them,' she snapped, turning her head away. In fact looking at any part of him was a bad idea, though unless she wanted to appear extremely odd she had no option. 'This might be a joke to you,' she remonstrated severely, 'but how do you think I'd have felt if I'd had your death on my conscience? Huh, I don't suppose you even thought of that, did you?' The hot, impassioned words tumbled out of her. 'No, of course not, you were too busy being Action Man. Talk about grandstanding!' She gave a disgusted snort.

It was one of life's injustices, she reflected bitterly, that men got to do all the glamorous action things and were then patted on the back and told what marvellous chaps they were. While women, because they were delicate and frail creatures, got to wait at home, look after the babies and go prematurely grey.

If Tom ever wanted to do something rash and life-threatening she was going to go with him. It didn't seem likely her resolve would be put to the test; if anything like that came up Tom would most probably delegate someone else to take care of it—which was the sensible thing to do.

You wouldn't catch Tom rushing into burning buildings for a cat; he would have, quite correctly, left it to a properly qualified person.

Actually, when you thought about it, have-a-go heroes were a bit of a liability.

Katie was disturbed to discover Nikos was looking at her rather too intently. 'You were scared for me?' he said, in the shocked manner of someone who had just made an extraordinary discovery.

She strove to calm her laboured breathing. 'I was... concerned, as I would have been about anyone in the circumstances. Though it seems my fears were groundless. You seem to lead a charmed life,' she observed heavily.

Her resentful gaze had examined most aspects of his person and she could see no obvious signs of injury other than a bloody gash on his temple. Even if he had emerged unscathed she considered his composure after such an incident abnormal. What did it take to shake this man? Demanding to be kissed would most likely do it. It was almost worth putting the theory to the test...*almost*!

'That has been said of me,' Nikos conceded with one of his charming, high-voltage grins. 'I'm touched by your concern, but it is unnecessary, I was in no serious danger.'

Katie had a sudden flashback to that awful moment the window had blown out. The metallic taste of fear was once more strong in her mouth as she again experienced that creeping paralysis of dread.

'Are you all right?'

'What could be wrong?' She was beginning to think that maybe he was one of those peculiar men who indulged in extreme sports, the sort that got a kick from risking life and limb.

'I managed to locate the fire escape,' he went on to explain, 'thanks to Alexander who was sitting at the top of it crying. That is, I'm assuming this is Alexander.' He opened his shirt, revealing a good deal of bare chest in the process, and presented her with a large, dirty cat who, at the prospect of being clutched to his loving owner's bosom, stopped purring like a steam engine and spat furiously before leaping into space and disappearing into some bushes.

Katie began to laugh a little hysterically. 'Oh, that's Alexander, all right, he's one of a kind. I'm surprised he let you carry him.'

'He was not too keen on the idea at first,' Nikos conceded drily. 'But he came around to it in the end.' He rubbed his face and revealed in the process a long, nasty-looking scratch.

'That's a first, Alexander is not a very...*pliable* animal. The vet did say he might be a little less aggressive if I had him done, but I couldn't bring myself to do it.' Nikos's penetrating eyes held an expression that made her wonder if he didn't have a hormone issue of his own? The introduction of this possibility made her lose the plot for a second. It was hard to concentrate when illicit thrills were fizzing through your body.

'Done?' Nikos echoed, looking puzzled.

Katie slowed her breathing and told herself that a man who had just escaped from the jaws of death was not likely to have sex on his mind. She mimed a snipping action with her fingers—an action guaranteed to pour cold water on the flame of the most persistent male lust—and Nikos gave a very predictable male gulp in response.

'I don't want to be responsible for an explosion in the local cat population so I keep him in at night,' she told him matter-of-factly.

From Nikos's glazed expression she had the feeling this was more information than he wanted. Not that he looked *bored*, precisely, *more*... A little shudder snaked its way down her spine. Perhaps she was way off beam, maybe the thoughts of a sizzling kiss were still on her mind. But while they were standing here talking about cats she felt as though there was a silent conversation going on that had nothing to do with words and everything to do with the way his dark eyes were eating her up.

'Don't you think you should do up your shirt? You might catch cold,' she suggested huskily as her eyes returned for the umpteenth time to the expanse of hard-muscled torso. The olive-toned flesh looked silkily smooth and hard and was dusted across the widest part of his broad chest with a fine sprinkling of dark hair that thinned the nearer his waist it got. Her stomach gave a lazy somersault as she followed the directional arrows.

He laid a hand against his firmly muscled midriff. 'Actually I feel quite warm.' For one awful moment Katie though he was going to invite her to feel for herself—an invitation she would *obviously* have rejected? 'How about you?'

Katie dabbed her tongue to the tiny beads of sweat along her upper lip and drew a shaky sigh. This time there was no longer any doubt about the undertones in this innocent enquiry. If she'd felt more herself and less like a lustful stranger Katie would have confronted him about his inappropriate flirting…*flirting*, with its light, frivolous overtones, was actually far too light a term for the erotic verbal games he played.

'I'm fine,' she returned, throwing him a look that dared him to contradict her. 'I'm really sorry about your face.' *Really sorry that it's so damned beautiful,* she thought weakly.

'I'll survive.' He suddenly reached across and pulled a piece of blossom from her hair.

Like a hunted deer being stalked by a wolf, Katie backed up into the tree. Her heart was beating like a war drum as he placed a hand on the smooth trunk above her head. If he leaned any closer their bodies would be touching…the crushing pressure reached the point where her shallow, painful breaths were clearly audible.

'You weren't hurt or anything?' It didn't really matter

what she said, she just had to speak, not only to demonstrate that he hadn't disturbed or rattled her, but to banish the erotic images from her head.

It did neither; her weak, wispy voice sounded as though it came from a great distance away. As for being undisturbed, she was clearly insane! It was taking literally all of her will-power to prevent herself turning her cheek into the palm that remained close to her face.

'Mr Lakis, I really must insist that you come with us now. You need to be checked over. Your wife too.' The paramedic turned to Katie, who tried to gather her wits. 'I understand from your friend that you too were inside the building earlier.'

It took Katie several seconds to register what he was saying and who he was saying it to. 'Oh, yes, but I'm fine.' *Wife*, he had definitely said *wife*. Her alarmed blue eyes flew accusingly to Nikos's face; he returned an insouciant smile. 'I'm perfectly fine,' she gritted.

The sexual tension might have dissipated, but she sensed it was still there, waiting beneath the surface to bubble up given the right conditions… Katie resolved never to permit that to happen.

Dark eyes gleaming with mockery, Nikos continued to smile down into her wrathful features. 'Let's allow the doctors to decide that, shall we, *yineka mou*?'

'Your husband's right, it's always best to be on the safe side, and that was quite a tumble you took. Did you do any damage?'

'You fell?' Nikos inserted, for all the world as if he actually was a concerned husband.

'She went down like a stone,' the other man confirmed. 'It isn't exactly a good idea to enter a burning building,' he added, slanting Katie a wry look.

'You went back into the building?'

Bemused by his anger, Katie shook her head. 'No, I didn't.'

'She fell over before she could get there. That's quite a turn of speed you have there, Mrs Lakis. I wouldn't bet against you in the hundred metres,' he teased.

Nikos, who was regarding her with total incredulity, did not appear to share his amusement.

'I wasn't thinking,' Katie said in a small voice.

'Don't worry about it,' the paramedic advised kindly. 'People rarely do think when they know a loved one is trapped in a burning building. Ask any of the fire crew.'

Katie didn't know where to look—except *not* at Nikos!

'Katerina has always been an impulsive creature, haven't you, *yineka mou*?'

The satiric bite in his voice made Katie wince. She did her best to disguise her limp, but evidently not well enough.

'You've hurt yourself!' the paramedic exclaimed in concern before she'd taken a couple of steps. 'Hey,' he hailed, 'the lady here needs a stretcher.'

Katie laid a restraining hand on his arm. 'Please, no stretcher,' she appealed, shaking her head. 'I'd much prefer to walk and it's nothing serious.'

To her intense annoyance he looked towards Nikos, who presumably gave her request his husbandly seal of approval, because the guy walked away and left them to make their own way to the ambulance.

Unbelievable! If she had been his wife in the real sense of the word, admittedly a scenario about as likely as seeing a herd of flying pigs overhead, but had she been, she would definitely have challenged this outrageous sexist assumption that she needed permission…that she wasn't capable of making her decisions.

Oh, my goodness, wouldn't I just! she thought grimly.

Obeying another of those unwise *impulses*, Katie lifted her head and for a split second her eyes meshed with midnight-dark orbs. It was long enough to reveal Nikos seemed to be really steamed up. This struck Katie as particularly perverse; she was the one who'd been made to feel a total fool. How dared he go around telling everyone she was his wife? As for the image the guy had drawn so vividly of a woman pushed beyond reason by an overriding compulsion to save her man, she had thought she would die from sheer embarrassment!

'Lean on me,' Nikos wanted to throttle the woman, but felt obliged to put aside his natural inclinations and offer his assistance having watched her painfully hobble a few steps while maintaining the pretence every one didn't hurt her like hell.

'I'd prefer to crawl on my hands and knees.'

The air hissed through his clenched teeth as he exhaled. 'As you wish,' he replied stiffly.

He made no concessions to her injury as he strode off, not that Katie wanted or expected any, but the grim smile pinned on her lips got harder and harder to maintain with each step.

'So were you so frightened for me that you were willing to risk your life in a futile attempt to rescue me?' Nikos's dark, sardonic voice observed somewhere above her head.

Katie's spirits, already badly mauled, sank to knee-level. Her worst fears were confirmed. This was exactly what she'd been dreading—he'd thought about her crazy rescue bid and come to the conclusion she'd acted that way because she was nursing some burning passion for him. Maybe he half expected women to fall in love with him? And maybe that expectation was usually justified, an ironic voice in her skull suggested.

Actually, when you thought about it, it was quite funny.

Despite recognising the humorous potential of the situation Katie found herself unable to laugh or even smile. She was, however, seized by a desperate need to establish that she was not one of the worshipping masses.

'It wasn't like that...' She paused and gave a frustrated sigh; how could you explain away why you did something when you didn't know yourself? 'I didn't think…' she revealed lamely.

'That I never doubted,' he incised grimly. 'For the past seven years when I have thought of you at all it has been as a shrewd, hard-headed young woman who, despite an extraordinarily innocent exterior, is capable of bending the rules ruthlessly to get what she wants. In short, a woman well able to take care of herself.'

He exhaled and dragged a hand roughly through his dark hair. 'That is what I expected, you understand? A woman like you should know how to negotiate. But what do I get?' His revolted gaze came to rest on the top of her head, which had she been able to stand upright would have just topped his shoulder. *'You…!'* He shook his head and, with an expression of rampant exasperation, began to list the traits he had discovered her to possess. 'Not only are you opinionated to the point of derangement…' he choked.

Good grief, she thought, lifting her astonished eyes to his furious face. *I needn't have worried—he doesn't think I'm in love with him, he just thinks I'm crazy! Could be he's not far out,* she thought, contemplating the firm contours of his mouth with an expression of dreamy speculation.

'Do not interrupt!' he thundered, holding up his hand. 'You are sentimental and you possess no sense of self-preservation whatever. I am a patient man…' he revealed without a trace of irony.

Too late, Katie clamped her hand over her lips to prevent the gurgle of laughter escaping.

Nikos gave her a thunderous look as he visibly fought to retain control of his extremely volatile temper—only he didn't have a volatile temper. 'I have humoured you too long,' he announced forcefully.

'That's a laugh—' she began. She let out a strangled shriek when without warning he swept her up into his arms and strode off without a single word.

'Put me down this instant!' she hissed. His arms were muscular and extremely strong because, although Katie was slim, she was not a small woman and he barely seemed to register the burden he carried.

'What, and see you stagger along in that ridiculous manner?'

Silently seething and reduced to winding her arms around his neck to anchor herself, Katie allowed herself to be carried to the ambulance with as much dignity as she could muster—what choice did have?

Sadie was waiting at the steps. 'Why did you tell them I had been in the flat?' Katie demanded of her friend in a trembling undertone.

Sadie looked startled at her vehemence and followed them up the stairs. 'Sorry, but they asked.'

Katie felt a wave of remorse. 'Sorry, I didn't mean to take it out on you. That man,' she explained, glaring at Nikos's ear, 'is a manipulative snake.' Even his hair curled perfectly into the nape of his neck.

She held herself rigid while, apparently oblivious to her insult, Nikos deposited her on a seat and straightened with sensible caution considering the limited headroom.

'I wouldn't trust him as far as I could throw him—*less*, in fact!' she declared loudly.

Sadie shot a wary look in Nikos's direction and he in his turn returned her look with a smile of spectacular charm, which much to Katie's disgust had an immediate effect on Sadie. She melted like an ice cream on a warm day.

'A sexy snake.'

Sadie's sly remark earned her an amused grin from Nikos. 'Thank you,' he said, inclining his head. 'And may I say that a true English rose like yourself is much admired in my country?'

Katie shook her head as Sadie blushed. 'What a load of b—'

'Don't spoil it, Katie,' Sadie interrupted, casting her

friend an irritated glance. 'Do go on,' she begged Nikos with a throaty laugh.

Katie glared at her friend indignantly—she was flirting, and flirting pretty well. 'Has anyone ever told you that you're a sucker for a pretty face?'

'Frequently,' Sadie admitted. 'I'd better go,' she added as the ambulance crew began to display impatience to be off. 'Call me later.' She smiled at the paramedic who, after checking that his passengers didn't require anything, had taken a seat at the opposite side of the vehicle.

'I feel terrible leaving you to cope with all of this mess,' Katie fretted.

'You know me, I thrive on challenge,' Sadie replied, cheerily waving goodbye.

'Your friend is very nice.'

'She's just recovering from an extremely messy divorce. So leave her alone, the last thing she needs is some slick operator moving on her,' she warned him grimly.

'I can pass the time of day with a woman without contemplating sleeping with her, you know.'

Katie snorted and Nikos looked amused. 'I have never been in an ambulance before,' he remarked, looking around with interest as the door closed. 'Or even,' he added with a mock growl, 'made love in one.'

'Very funny.' No doubt tonight's events would be regurgitated for the amusement of his glitzy friends—with suitable witty additions—for many weeks to come. 'I suppose *you* ride around in gold-plated limousines.'

'No, as a matter of fact I fly my own helicopter when possible. So do you really think I have a pretty face?' he continued seamlessly.

Talk about anything you say being used in evidence!

'That was a figure of speech.' Actually his was not a pretty face, it was a formidably *beautiful* face. She didn't need to look to see his dark, fallen-angel features or be transfixed by the brooding sensuality of his sexy eyes and mouth—they were etched in her mind.

How, she puzzled, could something as basic as the arrangement of planes and angles of a face make it so…? She struggled for a term adequate to describe it—unforgettable was a term casually bandied about, but in this instance it was fully deserved. Her memory would never be free of the image, she acknowledged, looking down at her hands tightened into fists on her lap.

'If you continue to breathe like that the professionals—' Nikos glanced towards the uniformed figure who had left his seat opposite and was now talking to the driver '—will assume that you need oxygen.'

Katie was disconcerted to discover that his eyes were contemplating the rapid rise and fall of her breasts… actually, disconcerted didn't really cover the things that were happening to her body. Nikos had to have noticed at least one of them as his attention was riveted in one of the areas in question; her breasts felt tense and tender and her nipples were active in a pleasurably painful way.

It had reached the point where she couldn't be sure what shocking surprise her body was going to spring on her next. Even the things coming out of her mouth seemed to be bypassing her brain.

'Why did you tell them I'm you're wife?' she asked in a desperate attempt to divert his attention from her aching, brazen breasts.

'You *are* my wife.'

Her inability to dispute this made Katie scowl. 'Only when it suits you,' she pointed out tartly.

Somehow she doubted Nikos would have been so eager to recognise their relationship if she'd turned up at his place of work declaring to all and sundry that he was her husband! What she couldn't figure was why he'd carelessly gone public, in this admittedly limited way, now. The last thing he struck her as being was a careless man; quite the contrary, she was pretty sure he never did anything without a reason, but what reason?

Possibly his actions were simply designed to wind her up?

For the past seven years he had successfully managed to forget he had a wife so she could strike the possibility that he'd decided she was the perfect bride for him.

No, he was up to something.

'We may have gone through a ceremony and signed on the dotted line, but it takes more than a signature on a piece of paper to make me your wife!' she told him scornfully.

'So, what does it take...?'

Katie shuffled away to lessen the contact of his heavy thigh against her own. The action only increased the worrying air of smug triumph she sensed in him.

'It takes...oh, for goodness' sake, will you stop that?'

'Stop what?'

'Will you stop looking at...you know?'

'No.'

Katie gave a snort of exasperation; the innocent look sat very uncomfortably. 'Well, how would you like it if I kept looking at your...?' Content she'd made her point, and deeply embarrassed into the bargain, she decided it would be expedient to move quickly on.

Nikos, however, seemed in no hurry to do so. 'I think I would find it quite stimulating,' he said.

Taking a deep steadying breath, Katie gritted her teeth and doggedly refused to allow him to distract her. 'It takes...' she began.

'What does it take?' he prompted, his curiosity genuinely aroused by the wistful expression he saw flit across her delicate, fine-boned features.

Katie shook her head; she was not about to expose her idea of an ideal marriage to his cynical scorn.

'Do you think they might let us a share a room at the hospital?'

'I suppose in Greece that passes for a sense of humour?' She gave a disdainful sniff and tried to stop herself coughing. 'Just for the record, I'm not sharing a room with you and I'm not staying in any hospital.'

Nikos shook his head. 'Did nobody ever tell you it's dangerous to tempt fate?'

CHAPTER SEVEN

'MARRIED?' the on-call radiographer, or Clare, as she had introduced herself, glanced towards Nikos. 'Yes, of course you are,' she said, not without a hint of envy. 'Date of birth...?' Katie gave it and the older woman checked the details on the form and nodded. 'Is there any possibility you are pregnant?'

She stood with her pen in her hand waiting for Katie's response. Katie, aware of Nikos's very interested presence beside her, felt her face flush. After a lengthy pause she shook her head and mumbled an indistinct, 'No, there isn't.'

The radiographer obviously misunderstood her hesitation. 'If you've any doubts?'

'I've no doubt at all,' Katie responded firmly. 'I can't possibly be pregnant. I haven't...' she choked.

'Oh, I see...' The radiographer nodded understandingly and shot a speculative look in Nikos's direction. 'So long as you're sure.'

'We have been living apart,' Katie was dismayed to hear him suddenly volunteer glibly. Equally suddenly he picked her hand up from where it lay twisted with its partner on her lap. With a tender smile he raised it to his lips. 'We are only recently reunited.'

His words and the fervent kiss he planted on her open palm managed to hint at a lovers-parted-and-reunited story of epic proportions.

The radiographer was clearly a big fan of a happy ending. 'Oh, isn't that lovely?' she sighed soulfully. 'You just wait here a moment, Mrs Lakis, and I'll be right back.'

The instant she was gone Katie snatched her tingling

hand away and wiped it across her lap vigorously, as though she could wipe his touch away.

'Was that charade really necessary?' she enquired icily. It seemed he couldn't resist any opportunity to provoke and embarrass her. Or maybe, she mused scornfully, he just couldn't let the implied slur on his manhood stand. Yeah, that would be right.

'So you're not sleeping with Tom?'

Katie stiffened defensively as his question took her off guard. 'That's none of your business, but if I was,' she added confidently, '*I* certainly wouldn't be stupid enough to get pregnant.'

Though she wasn't as a rule a judgmental person, she had always found it hard to understand how in a day and age when contraception was so readily available people still fell pregnant unintentionally—though the *falling* was part of the self-deception as far as she was concerned; there was nothing accidental about it.

'Maybe, maybe not...people in the grip of passion do not always think logically.'

'Rubbish.' One dark brow lifted at her forceful denunciation. 'There's absolutely no excuse for neglecting to take basic precautions.'

Katie frowned to hear herself sound so self-righteous and dogmatic...it was the sort of uncharacteristic response he brought out in her. He said night and she was almost falling over herself to screech day.

An enigmatic half-smile touched the corners of Nikos's wide, passionate mouth as he observed the flare of panic in her eyes.

'So you don't think that the dizzy heights of passion could make a person, could make *you*, forget?' His heavy lids lifted and Katie found herself captured and as helpless as a butterfly caught on a cruel pin by his dark gaze. 'Forget your own name, where you begin and your lover ends...?' he persisted throatily.

His rough velvet voice was describing a situation that was beyond her understanding, but one that held a dangerous appeal. Just listening to his sweetly insidious drawl made her feel hot and cold at the same time, and increased that tight, achy feeling that had been a more or less constant presence low in her belly all night.

The way his knowledgeable eyes were scanning her face made Katie, bitterly ashamed of her body's wanton response, shift uncomfortably in her seat.

'Forget the most basic precautions? Do me a favour,' she scoffed stubbornly.

'You cannot visualise yourself in a situation like that?'

'No!' Katie gritted through clenched teeth as she tried very hard not to allow the images he spoke of to crystallise in her mind. Even though she tried very hard some images filtered through her mental block; they were of limbs entwined, warm brown skin gleaming with sweat, fractured gasps and soft moans. She was hard put not to moan herself.

Nikos was beginning to think that the favour that would most benefit her would come from someone who could wipe that smug look of superiority from her face—his narrowed gaze homed in on the soft contours of her full lips—and why should that person not be him?

The voice of reason in his head immediately provided at least half a dozen legitimate reasons why it should not. Despite this, the idea, however ill advised, lingered on.

'No matter how sophisticated society becomes, mother nature has built in some very efficient safety systems into the human design that will ensure the continuation of the species despite our best attempts to foil her.' In a voice that was all honeyed temptation and earthy suggestion, he expanded his theory into territory Katie found even more uncomfortable, yet despite this she found herself perversely hanging on his every word. 'It is not by accident that we are intoxicated, that sense and reason are suspended in the heat of passion.

'Men,' he proclaimed confidently, 'are programmed to impregnate and woman are programmed to bear children.' He shrugged and studied her shocked face; it seemed to Katie that the silver flecks in his eyes glittered like stars in a night sky. 'You can't fight against basic instincts, *pethu mou*.'

She tried to escape but her restless gaze was repeatedly drawn back to his; a stab of sexual longing so fierce it robbed her of breath lanced through her body.

Katie shook her head. 'You can't talk like that,' she gasped in an agonised whisper. The men she knew didn't casually discuss impregnation in hospital waiting rooms.

'You find my frankness offensive? Such things make you squeamish?'

Offended? She was terrified.

'I am not squeamish. I just don't think this is the appropriate time or place for talking about such things,' she told him repressively. Unfortunately Nikos was not so easily repressed.

'Sex is not a subject for open discussion?'

'Not between people who are virtually strangers.'

'So if I was Tom you would feel comfortable discussing sex.'

Katie took a deep, infuriated breath. 'Tom and I do not discuss sex,' she yelled.

'Mrs Lakis...?'

Katie spun around to find the radiographer standing there.

'We're ready for you now.'

Her ankle was declared a nasty sprain, which they strapped with a stretchy support bandage and advised her to keep elevated. The doctor said he was satisfied that she had not sustained any damage to her lungs, though he did suggest Katie might like to stay in overnight to be observed.

To her relief when she politely but firmly refused the invitation he wasn't too perturbed.

'The doctor should be finished with your husband in a few minutes,' the nice nurse who had attended her promised, showing her to a waiting area.

I can hardly wait.

Katie had caught sight of her reflection in a plate-glass door so wasn't surprised that on the way there she was the focus of a number of curious stares.

Not to put too fine a point on it, she looked scary!

It was hard to tell what the original colour of Sadie's once lovely dress was and there were several rips in the long skirt that revealed more than was decent of her long, grubby legs. Though she'd had the opportunity to wash the worst of the dirt from her face and hands, what she longed for most was to soak in a lovely hot bath until the acrid smoky smell that seemed to have penetrated pore-deep was gone.

'I feel awful for asking, but I don't suppose you've got any change for the phone, have you? I didn't exactly come prepared,' she explained with a rueful glance down at her ruined outfit.

Katie waited until the helpful nurse was out of sight before she headed for the pay phone she'd spotted in the foyer. First she phoned Tom; he wasn't at home and he wasn't answering his cell phone. She was about to leave him a message, but thought better of it…there was nothing he could do and telling him about the fire would only alarm him unnecessarily.

Next she rang Sadie's mobile number.

'I was starting to think they were keeping you in,' Sadie said, sounding tired but pretty upbeat, which in the circumstances said a great deal for her powers of endurance.

Sadie got the bad news over with first.

'Your flat's a write-off. The good news is they managed to contain the fire to the top floor. The rest of the house is all right, barring some smoke damage in the hall and down the stairs. I'm staying with the Jameses next door tonight, they said you're quite welcome to kip down on their sofa. I've got the spare room.'

'Say thanks to them from me, but actually I can't face the journey back.' The hospital was a fifteen-mile trip from the village and she was ready to drop; in fact, remaining upright was difficult. 'I'm just going to get a taxi to the nearest hotel and sleep for a week.'

'Fair enough, see you tomorrow?'

'Definitely,' Katie agreed. 'Sadie…I'm really sorry,' she added in a rush.

'God, we don't even know if it was your fault and I'm the one that didn't get around to refitting the fire alarms after the painters finished last month. Besides, nobody was hurt, that's the main thing, and I'm extremely well-insured,' she added cheerfully. 'So don't beat yourself up about it.'

It wasn't until she'd hung up that Katie realised she had no money for a taxi, hotel room or, for that matter, any more for the phone. *Don't panic, think about this calmly and logically,* she told herself.

So *logically* she had no money, and calmly she had no transport, her head hurt and she was dressed in revealing rags—Katie reckoned she was entitled to panic a little and to feel mildly despondent.

Maybe I should have taken up the offer of a hospital bed, she thought as she stepped into the reception area, a big densely carpeted open space that was divided by banks of greenery and seats—obviously meant to give a welcoming impression. The place, a hive of activity during the daytime, was, barring a few porters and sundry members of staff who were on their way somewhere in a hurry, almost completely deserted at this time of night.

Katie wasn't on her way anywhere. She wrapped her arms across her chest feeling incredibly conspicuous and rather lonely. Her adrenalin levels had dropped and the events of the evening were beginning to catch up on her with a vengeance.

'Here, take this.'

Startled out of her gloomy thoughts by the deep voice, Katie looked at the jacket being offered to her and then warily at the man himself.

He was as dishevelled as she was, his skin and clothes streaked with black, but unlike her he appeared supremely indifferent to the fact. It struck her as deeply unfair that, whereas torn clothes and messy hair made her look like a scarecrow, they lent him an indefinable edge of mystery and danger…mean, moody and macho…nobody was going to overlook him in a crowd!

She was inclined to think that if you stripped this man of his wealth, status and even his clothes he wouldn't lose his infuriating imperious air of command.

Katie raised her eyes with a jerk to his face feeling, and probably looking, as guilty as any nicely brought-up girl would caught in the act of mentally stripping a man—*make a note for future reference: do not think naked around Nikos*—but then no matter how things turned out she wouldn't be around him for very much longer.

This reflection ought to have made her feel upbeat—but somehow a heavy feeling had settled over her.

'You are shivering,' he observed with a frown.

Katie looked again at the jacket; she thought of refusing it and then decided this would be an empty gesture and, besides, she didn't want to risk being arrested for indecent exposure!

'Yes, I am. Thank you.' She slid the jacket over her hunched shoulders, and drew it around herself. It still held the warmth of his body; she found this second-hand warmth disturbingly intimate. 'My dress has a little more ventilation than was intended.'

'I could say I hadn't noticed, but I'd be lying.'

Katie shot him a wary glance but his enigmatic expression was unrevealing—maybe that was just as well.

'Sit?' he suggested, nodding towards a seated area.

Katie shook her head. 'Hospitals at night are strange, don't you think?' Her restless glance took in the big empty area. 'Almost spooky,' she heard herself babble.

'I thought you'd gone.'

Katie didn't tell him that that had been her plan.

'Have you contacted Tom?'

She shook her head. 'I tried to.' Not so very hard, a voice in her head suggested drily. 'He's not picking up, but it sounded as if he was in for an all-night session, didn't it? He could very well be in the middle of sensitive negotiations,' she elaborated, 'so it's probably better I don't bother him.'

'I don't think many men would consider it a *bother* to drop whatever they were doing if their woman had just escaped death.' The contemptuous curl of his upper lip seemed to be a reflection of Nikos's opinion of any man who wouldn't rush to the side of their woman.

Katie was annoyed that she felt impelled to defend her absent fiancé.

'And Tom would!' she began. 'Escaped *death*...' she added, frowning. 'Isn't that a tad over-dramatic?' Her light laughter trailed away as she tried to imagine Tom calling her *his woman* in that way, and if he had she would probably have laughed.

When Nikos used the term it didn't sound funny. It must be the accent—men with exotic, sexy accents could get away with saying things that a native speaker could not. It went without saying that she didn't want anyone to call her *his woman*; it was sort of dated, sexist stuff—the sort of things the man that her grandfather had picked out for her mother would have used.

She concluded that his accent must be responsible for

the shivery sensations she experienced every time he was around.

'Possibly.' He conceded her words with a careless shrug of his broad shoulders. The flimsy nature of his shirt made it difficult not to notice how his taut muscles flexed and bulged through the fine material. 'But nevertheless I think you should let Tom decide that for himself.'

Katie's lips tightened; his persistence, not to mention his perfect musculature, was beginning to annoy her.

'Can't you wait until the morning to tell him what an awful creature he's got mixed up with?' she taunted.

'Actually I was thinking of how I would feel in his place.'

Katie flushed, not enjoying the sensation of being quietly put in her place. 'I suppose that must have taken quite a stretch of your no doubt limited imagination.'

'Theos!' Anger lent his dark, taut features a menacing cast.

'And I suppose *you* would walk away from an important business negotiation if your girlfriend needed you. That's *really* likely.' This was the sort of man who put personal relationships way down his list of priorities.

A wave of weakness suddenly hit her; it was so strong she swayed. Nikos, whose simmering anger had left him the moment he'd taken in the white-faced exhaustion in her face, took her by the arm.

'Sit!' he urged strongly. The woman was clearly unfit to take care of herself. He wondered why Tom let her out alone!

Katie complied, reasoning it would be a lot more embarrassing to fall on her face than follow his direction. Pride had its place but you had to know when to swallow it. She sat for a moment with her eyes closed, waiting for the awful weakness to pass. To her relief Nikos let her be.

'I'm a little tired.'

Nikos slanted her a veiled look through half-lowered lids.

'I find it strange that you feel obliged to apologise for behaviour that needs no apology but not for insults you throw so indiscriminately at me.' He shook his head when she opened her mouth to respond.

'Hush!' he urged, pressing a finger to her parted lips. 'We will not squabble. I am not so unimaginative that I cannot see you are at the end of your tether. As for what I would do, we are not talking about me.'

Not talking, thinking or fantasising about, which was something she really ought to bear in mind! Unconsciously she ran the back of her hand across her lips where he had touched.

'I just thought that Tom isn't going to lose any sleep over what he doesn't know about. Besides,' she added brightly, 'he knows I don't need him to hold my hand every time something goes wrong.'

'You are a tough, independent woman, then?' Nikos asked, sounding amused.

Katie's eyes narrowed. Her want-to-make-something-of-it? look was weak, but strong enough to make her opinion of his condescension known.

'If you're asking if I'm quite capable of taking care of myself, then,' she told him proudly, 'yes, I am. Do you have a problem with that?'

He would prefer his women clingy and needy; that went without saying. The sort that would tell him at frequent intervals how big, strong and marvellous he was, and never, *ever* disagree with him! In short, women who would not upset his theory that the world revolved around him, she concluded scornfully.

'Does Tom?' he fired back smoothly.

Katie waved her tastelessly large diamond ring at him. 'Quite obviously not.'

'Maybe you are more circumspect around him?' he suggested drily.

'Around *Tom* I can relax,' she breathed, closing her eyes

and imagining herself in his undemanding company. With Tom she never felt stressed or under pressure or…*excited*?

Her eyes shot wide open; where did that come from?

'But not around me?'

Katie laughed; she couldn't help herself. It was such a ludicrous idea: relax with Nikos! She could more readily imagine falling asleep on top of an active volcano! But then, she mused as her eyes moved over his tall, elegant figure, he did have something of a volcano's explosive qualities…and he was liable to erupt for no apparent reason.

'Do I look that stupid?' If ever there was an invitation, this was it.

Katie heaved a sigh and squared her shoulders, steeling herself for the inevitable scathing riposte…it didn't come. In fact the strange, tense silence between them stretched on and on…

He had stilled to the point of seeming not to breathe at all as his restless dark eyes got as far as her face and didn't move. An expression she couldn't decipher flickered across his taut face; it was only there for a moment, but this was long enough to unsettle her completely.

'No.'

After the build-up she'd been expecting something a bit more—memorable than that.

'You didn't answer my question.' Except with a question—he seemed to be good at that. 'Do you have a problem with strong women?'

Nikos shrugged. 'Strength is not an issue. My relationships with women are rarely competitive either physically or intellectually.'

Katie's contempt increased. In other words he picked them weak, thick and great in bed. *Just as well I'm not after the job because I don't qualify in any of the above.*

'Some women feel there is a need to sacrifice their femininity in order to compete on an equal footing with men;

that is their choice. I just happen not to find them particularly attractive. I admire women that manage to succeed but do not try to be one of the boys.'

'Are you calling me unfeminine?' she demanded hotly.

'I would hardly categorise you as a high-flyer who is anxious to compete with men on their own terms.'

Why, the patronising—!

'Are you leaving your job before or after the wedding?' he wondered with a guileless smile.

Katie caught her breath. You had to hand it to the man—he could deliver insults with a smile better than anyone she had ever met.

'I'm not leaving at all. My job may not be high-powered but I happen to enjoy it,' she told him with frigid dignity.

'Really?' One dark eyebrow lifted. 'Tom led me to believe you could not wait to leave...'

'I haven't told Tom yet,' she interrupted tightly.

'Do you tell Tom *anything*?'

'My relationship with Tom is none of your business.'

'Actually it is very much my business.'

'Only because you're an insufferably, interfering...' Lips compressed, eyes glittering with suppressed frustration, Katie bit back the rest of her tirade; this was neither the time nor place for a slanging match, especially one she was likely to lose.

'Don't you think Tom is capable of making his own decisions without you to shove him in the right direction? Not that you could,' she added quickly. She lifted her chin. 'Tom is his own man!' she declared proudly.

'I'm sure Tom is more than capable of making his own decisions when he is in possession of all the facts...once he has them I will be more than happy to abide by his decision.'

'It's not the facts, it's the way you present them.'

'Then you present them in the manner you feel shows you in the kindest light; I have no objections. Even if Tom accepts his wealth has nothing to do with your desire to be his wife.' His expression made it clear he was a lot less gullible. 'That does not alter the fact you are not free to marry him.'

'I could be if you weren't such a stubborn, malicious...' She heaved several steadying breaths; she would not resort to name-calling. 'Why should I marry Tom when apparently I'm already married to a billionaire?'

Nikos, who seemed prepared for her comment, totally misinterpreted her throw-away sarcasm.

'Before the pound signs start flashing before your eyes I will draw to your attention the fact that the pre-nuptial agreement Harvey had me sign works both ways. I've checked, Harvey knows his business, it's watertight. Sorry, but I'm not your golden goose. What's wrong?' he asked as the colour seeped from her skin.

Katie, her eyes bright pools of shimmering anger stared up at him. Incredibly his bafflement seemed genuine...how could anyone possibly insult a person like that and not realise it might offend?

She began to slide his jacket off her shoulders. 'Don't let me keep you,' she said pointedly.

'Don't be foolish,' he retorted impatiently. 'You are cold, I'm not. This is a foolish gesture.'

Katie shrugged and let the jacket slip to the ground. 'Maybe I want to make a foolish gesture.'

'Now you're just being ridiculous,' he gritted, bending to retrieve the garment from the carpeted floor. His colour was heightened when he took his seat; the twist of his sensual lips was overtly contemptuous.

'That's your fault,' she blurted resentfully.

One supremely eloquent dark brow twitched as his expressive eyes swept over her face. 'This I have to hear,' he remarked, throwing the jacket casually across one shoulder. 'You were saying?'

Katie flushed. 'There's no point saying anything because

no matter what I say you'll just twist it,' she announced mutinously.

'In other words your accusations have no foundation.' Before she could protest he replaced his jacket over her shoulders and, keeping a grip on each lapel, jerked her gently towards him. Katie was overpoweringly conscious of his strength; she breathed in his warm male scent and felt uncomfortably giddy.

He bent his head towards her. 'No matter how outrageously unpleasant you become,' he imparted softly, 'I am not leaving you alone.'

'So you'll just call me an avaricious grasping bitch!' To her intense dismay Katie felt her eyes fill with weak tears.

Nikos looked into the swimming blue pools, an expression of genuine surprise stamped across his handsome features. 'I said nothing of the sort!' he ejaculated.

'You accused me of wanting to screw you for some nice fat divorce settlement!' She breathed wrathfully. 'For your information I wouldn't take my bus fare off you,' she added tremulously.

How, she wondered, could you detest someone so much yet find you wanted to lay your head against his chest and cry? Why in the circumstances would anybody in their right mind seek comfort and safety in the arms of their enemy? It was inexplicable and extremely scary, she concluded, staring with a dazed expression at the broad expanse that filled her with the strangest yearning.

As he surveyed her downcast features the harsh lines of Nikos's face softened. 'I did not intend to offend you, Katerina. Let us stop arguing, you're not well.'

'What's this—Greek chivalry?'

He picked up on her scorn but reacted with curiosity, not injured pride. 'You doubt such a thing exists?'

'After meeting you—*yes*!'

Surprisingly her acid retort made him laugh, then as his

appraisal of her weary, strained features continued his expression sobered once more. 'Let's be practical.'

When am I anything else? Katie thought with a spurt of revolt.

'What actually are your plans?'

Did she have any? She shrugged. 'Hopefully I won't be reduced to sleeping on a park bench.'

'What's this—British humour?' Despite her determination to be angry with him, Katie was amused to hear him cleverly use her own format against her. Whatever else was wrong with him, the man did have a quick wit and clever tongue—far too clever, she brooded darkly. A conversation with him had more dips and bends than a roller coaster.

'You doubt such a thing exists?' she quipped.

'What can I say without insulting a person's cultural heritage?'

Katie flushed at the subtle reprimand, then got even more worried when it occurred to her that he might have imagined there were xenophobic overtones in her earlier gibe. She frowned as she tried to recall whether what she had said could be construed that way.

'Have you ever actually met any Greeks other than myself?'

'Yes. As a matter of fact I've lived with one.' She was pleased to see her enigmatic reply disconcert him; if she had been better acquainted with him she would have been even more surprised.

'Does Tom know about this?'

Katie gave him a sunny, composed smile. 'Yes, he does.'

'I suppose this failed relationship explains your antipathy to me.'

'Did I say I had a failed relationship?'

'I naturally assumed as you're not in it any longer...'

'Well, you assumed wrong,' she replied, her eyes locked to his. She hadn't intended to make her reply vague, but now that she thought about it having Nikos imagine she had a colourful past did not seem such a bad idea.

'As a matter of fact it was a *beautiful* relationship.' The taunting tone suddenly died from her voice and her eyes softened. 'Very beautiful,' she revealed in a tone of deep, ineffable sadness. 'I doubt if I'll ever have a relationship quite like it again.' Unless she had a daughter of her own one day?

'Then your antipathy to me…'

'Is solely due to the fact that you're an offensive, malicious, detestable man.'

In the thunderous silence that followed her pronouncement Katie started to regret being so mean. *I haven't even asked if he's all right,* she thought, glancing guiltily towards the wound on his forehead. It was barely visible through the heavy swathe of hair that had fallen across his forehead.

'I didn't mean to offend you,' she added when he didn't respond. 'Well, I did, but not— Oh, for heaven's sake, don't sulk!' she blurted out in frustration. She waited for the inevitable ice to filter into his expression and wondered if there was a medical condition that could account for what her tongue was doing.

'Relax, Katerina,' he advised. 'I'm not offended.'

She gave a sigh of relief. 'Good. What did the doctor say?'

'My chest is clear.'

Your chest is perfect, Katie thought. 'That's excellent,' she said gravely.

'And the X-ray of my skull was as it should be. They insisted on putting a stitch or two in my head,' he admitted in a casual manner.

'One or two?' Katie echoed doubtfully. 'It looks more to me…' Without thinking, she reached out to lift the concealing hair from the wound. Before she touched him long brown fingers curled over her own. A bolt of neat electricity sizzled along her raw nerve endings.

'Will you not take my word?' He gave a humourless smile. He seemed a little tense…but then there was a lot of it about, she thought, swallowing a bubble of hysteria. 'No, of course you won't.'

'I only wanted to see if you're all right.'

Nikos dismissed her concern with a terse shake of his head. 'The amount of stitches is of no consequence.'

He brought her hand down but didn't release it immediately; instead he turned it over and ran his thumb across her open palm.

'You have pretty hands.' He looked as if he was almost as surprised to hear himself say this as she was.

Katie's eyes lingered on his long, tapering fingers. His were strong, expressive hands and her tummy fluttered again.

'Thank you, so do you.'

She sensed some of the tension slip away from him and, though his lips twitched, he didn't respond to her comment.

'You know, I think we can do a little better than that park bench.'

Although the physical contact had disturbed her she felt a twinge of regret when he released her hand. She tried to gather her straying wits. 'What do you mean…?'

'I mean I have a suite at the Hall Hotel.'

He would, of course—staying in anything less than a five-star hotel would obviously be beneath his dignity, and the Hall was the only five-star hotel in the area.

'That's you sorted, then.'

Nikos gave a heavy sigh and looked impatient. '*Theos*, you are hard work,' he observed tersely. 'We're both tired…'

'Which is no excuse to snap.'

A nerve in his lean cheek began to pump. 'So kind of you to remind me of *my* manners.'

'I get the feeling that doesn't happen too often.' *More's the pity,* she thought, sending him a sour look.

He signalled his disapproval of the interruption with the faintest twist of his lips. 'I was about to say that I'm quite willing to take your extreme reluctance to accept my help as read? It will save a lot of time and frayed tempers in the long run. If anyone asks I'll swear you fought me tooth and nail. You hate me, I'm arrogant, you'd prefer to sleep on a park bench…blah…blah…' he drawled.

She shot him a look of intense dislike. 'I know this confirms my boring predictability, but I *would* prefer to sleep on a park bench!' she declared.

'Well done!' he congratulated her. 'The first step in correcting our faults is accepting you have a problem.'

'Once you go away I won't have a problem.' *If you overlook my penniless and homeless condition.* Heavens, what was she going to do if he took her at her word…?

'Don't make a song and dance about this. You can't stay here, you have no money. I, on the other hand, have—'

'Too much money.'

'Some people might think so,' he conceded, 'but actually I was thinking of a spare bed and a taxi which should arrive any moment.'

'*Spare* bed?'

'Sorry if you thought otherwise, but it has been a long day…' he explained apologetically.

Katie blushed fierily at the silky innuendo in his voice. She gathered the jacket and her dignity around herself as best she could.

'You won't know I'm there,' she promised grimly.

Nikos regarded the top of her dark head with a twisted smile. 'That I very much doubt, *agape mou,*' he drawled.

She pretended not to hear the endearment.

CHAPTER EIGHT

KATIE sniffed a few of the luxury bath products provided and, selecting one that had a tang of rosemary, she poured it into the water.

She inhaled deeply, enjoying the scent from the pungent-smelling oil in the steamy air. She gave a deep sigh as she slid slowly into the hot water. It was bliss.

She lost track of time as she lay there, drifting in every sense of the word. The delightful idyll was only spoiled when there was a loud knock on the door.

Katie groaned and slid under the water to block out the noise; fronds of water-darkened hair floated on the surface like exotic petals above her head. When she emerged, wet hair plastered to her face, the knocking was louder and accompanied by a voice. She wiped the moisture from her face with her hand and grimaced.

'Are you all right, Katerina? If you don't answer me I shall be forced to come in!'

He would too.

This was a situation fraught with dangerous possibilities…which no doubt accounted for the dramatic increase in her pulse-rate.

Katie bit her lip and blew a section of frothy suds from her arm, watching as individual bubbles detached themselves and began to float across the room.

'It's locked!' she shouted, hoping he'd go away.

If she hoped he'd go away, why then did she have this image in her head of being joined in the water by a sleekly muscled male body…? Why even as she spoke was she seeing water sliding over powerful shoulders…?

She almost certainly didn't want answers to these questions.

There was a short silence. 'A locked door is not an obstacle to a determined man,' he told her, sounding irritated but a lot more relaxed than he had done before she'd spoken. 'So if you are not unconscious answer me.'

Katie watched the bubble that had travelled the farthest ping on a mirrored surface. 'What do you want?' she called crossly.

'Do you want anything from room service? I'm ordering some supper.'

Her stomach responded to the offer with a hungry growl. 'No.'

'You hardly ate anything at dinner.'

'And whose fault is that...?'

'You ought to have something,' Nikos persisted, choosing to ignore her indignant accusation.

'What are you going to do, force-feed me?' She winced at the sound of her own voice. *God, this is starting to sound more and more like a playground squabble.* One of them had to start acting like a grown-up. 'Actually...Nikos...' she began tentatively. Why was it so hard for her to say his name? 'I wouldn't mind a sandwich? Nikos...?' she called, but there was no response. She shrugged; he obviously hadn't hung around.

Katie sank back down into the scented water but found it impossible to recapture her relaxed mood, so after washing her long hair until it was squeaky clean she climbed out of the roll-top bath. As she reached for a towel she caught a glimpse of herself in a mirror—how could she not? The ceiling was about the only place in the bathroom that didn't have a reflective surface.

She barely registered the fleeting image she had of the tall girl with long, slim legs, flat belly and firm, fairly full breasts with small pouting nipples that stood out darkly against pale honey skin. She picked a large soft towel from the pile on the vanity unit and was about to dry herself when an impulse made her turn and rub some of the condensation from the nearest mirror.

Towel still in her hands, she extended one leg in front of her and pointed her toes, watching the effect of her balletic pose in the mirror. Thoughtfully she replaced her foot on the tiled floor then turned, viewing her body critically from several angles. How, she wondered, would a stranger view this body? Would they notice that her hip bones were too bonily prominent or detect that, viewing from this angle, you could see that her right breast was just fractionally fuller than the left?

She ran her fingers slowly down the damp flat contours of her belly; the sensitised nerves in her abdomen quivered under her touch. She found herself staring into her own eyes…they were darkened, alien, the pupils dilated. She shivered, not from cold because her skin was hot to the touch.

'Oh, my goodness!' she gasped, wiping a shaking hand across her lips, which appeared pinker and fuller than usual—*as if I'd just been kissed. Who am I kidding? It's no stranger's eyes I'm trying to see myself through, but a very specific pair of eyes—inky-dark fathomless eyes.*

It was bad she was thinking about Nikos looking at her naked, but infinitely worse was the inescapable fact she was getting seriously aroused thinking about him doing so!

Shaking with reaction, she covered her shamefully engorged nipples with her crossed arms and stumbled towards the washbasin; gulping, she turned on the cold tap. The cold water she splashed on her face did clear her head but not her deeply troubled thoughts.

I'm about to marry one man and I'm thinking this way about another.

'What does that say about me?' she demanded of the image in the mirror. The fact that she was actually married to the object of her lustful fancies was not, considering the exceptional circumstances, relevant.

Maybe it was time to admit what she had with Tom was not a basis for a lifelong commitment? She shook her head, rejecting the idea. Friendship and respect lasted longer than lust—this inevitably led her thoughts full circle back to Nikos.

'I will not let him do this to me!' she gritted out loud. Only an idiot would want a spectacular burst of showy fireworks when they could have a steady, slow-burning flame. But did she?

Shaking the excess moisture off her face, she took a deep breath and began to rub herself vigorously with a towel. Long before she'd finished her skin was pink and tingling.

When Katie went back through to her bedroom the door to the sitting room shared by the two bedrooms in the large, luxurious suite was open. She couldn't hear any signs of life beyond it, but just in case she tiptoed quietly towards it with the intention of surreptitiously shutting it. She'd feel safer with a visible barrier between them...*but would he,* the sly voice in her head wondered...*if he knew what you were thinking?*

That was never going to happen!

Pretending she wasn't attracted to him was not going to work any more—actually it never had worked particularly well to begin with—neither could she blame it on the heightened emotions surrounding the fire. The truth was every time she looked at him she was overwhelmed by a mindless hunger with an emphasis on the mindless. Lust was something she could deal with, she told herself without a great deal of conviction.

If only, she thought wistfully as she grasped the door handle, Nikos could be as easily shut out of her thoughts. As part of her new honesty policy she acknowledged it was going to take a lot more than two inches of polished mahogany to accomplish that—*yes, that's going to take a bit of good old-fashioned self-control,* she told herself sternly, *so stop acting as if you don't have any choice about this!*

'There's always a choice!' Katie grimaced to hear the lack of conviction in her voice—*once more with feeling, girl!* 'There's *always* a choice...?'

She frowned and leaned her weight against the door, which, only half closed, had come to an abrupt halt. She grunted softly and gave a shove just as the obstacle revealed itself to be a six-feet-five-in-his-bare-feet obstacle!

Her stomach dipped dramatically as she angled a dismayed look up at his lean, imposing features.

Oh, heavens! Not only could she not get him out of her thoughts, her assumption she could physically shut him out was proving to be optimistic as well!

'Sorry, I didn't see you there.' She smiled tensely as he opened the door fully, and tightened the belt on the calf-length hotel robe. As befitted an up-market hotel, the robe in question was as sumptuously rich as the décor; in fact it was so fluffy and comforting it was hard to tell she had a waist.

Only Katie didn't feel particularly comforted wearing it; it wasn't the provocative nature of this modest get-up that bothered her, but what she was—or rather what she *wasn't*—wearing underneath!

Her glance skimmed over Nikos in what she hoped was a casual way, not likely to be misconstrued as an I-want-to-rip-your-clothes-off sort of way! It revealed that, like herself, he had used the time to bathe, but unlike her he did not have to rely on the robes the hotel supplied. He had changed into casual light-coloured jeans and a polo shirt in a slightly darker silky fabric.

This relaxed version of Nikos was equally devastatingly attractive as the formal one.

'Were you talking to yourself...?'

Katie, lips clamped tight, shook her head vigorously.

One dark brow quirked. 'I thought I heard something.'

'I must have been thinking out loud...'

His lips quivered faintly. 'But not talking to yourself.'

His mockery made her want to hit him, which was not a civilised response, but somehow civilised was hard to achieve around Nikos.

'Sorry if it disturbed you. Goodnight?' she added with more hope than expectation of him taking the hint. He was not big on taking hints.

'You thought I was asleep, perhaps?'

A perfectly innocent question, but something about the gleam in his slightly narrowed eyes made Katie suspect some sort of trap in his seemingly innocuous words.

Nikos had found that many women with expertly applied make-up were almost unrecognisable when seen without it; this was not the case with Katerina. A searching scrutiny of her freshly scrubbed features had revealed a complexion that was flawless, her full, wide lips were a delightful deep pink, the only flaw in fact was the faint bruised bluish shadows beneath her wide-spaced, incredibly blue eyes. Did she not sleep enough? The thought of what she did when she should be sleeping brought a harsh, uncompromising frown to his brow.

'Asleep?' she repeated, wary and resentful of the stern look of disapproval he was giving her. 'I hadn't really thought about it.'

'Then I really can't account for it.'

'Account for what?'

Still frowning, Katie turned, her eyes following the direction the sharp tilt of his dark head indicated. She almost groaned out loud when she saw what he was showing her. The large gilt-framed mirror above the queen-sized bed was clearly visible from the other room through the door. It must have given him a perfect view of her approaching the door.

'You looked as if you were trying not to disturb anyone, like a little mouse.'

Katie, recalling the furtive way she'd crept across the room, felt a hot tide of mortification wash over her skin.

'One would be excused,' he continued, 'for thinking you didn't want me to hear you.'

Katie bit her lip; the rat was enjoying her discomfort, she could see it in his eyes. *Just so long as he doesn't find mine equally revealing.* The thought sent a shudder slithering down her spine. She swallowed.

'I said you wouldn't know I was here,' she reminded him.

'So you did. You are so considerate,' he murmured with palpable insincerity. He nudged the door wider with his shoulder and his features hardened. 'Except when you let me think you've passed out in the bath.'

She was startled by the unexpected comment and her eyes flew to his face. 'You didn't think that.' Her scornful smile faded as their eyes locked, her own widened. '*Did you?* But I don't faint...'

A swift mental review of the events in question left her uneasily conscious that her refusal to respond to his calls just might have been interpreted that way by someone who was totally over-cautious.

'It was not such a great leap to make. Consider,' he suggested. 'You are obviously totally exhausted, you have had a traumatic experience...and of course I did not have that one vital piece of information which would have made me realise that my fears were groundless—you don't faint,' he observed with heavy sarcasm.

Katie tossed her head back and gave a combative smile, she'd show him that a totally exhausted—which in her book translated as 'you look like hell'—person was not going to meekly accept his lectures.

'Who do you think you are?'

'Your husband.'

For a moment Katie thought he really could read her

mind until common sense intervened and she reasoned that she must have spoken out loud.

'I take it the traumatic experience you are referring to is you showing up?' Her defiant shrug had a hint of desperation about it; though pitting her wits against Nikos was stimulating in a sticking-your-finger-in-an-electric-socket sort of way, it was also deeply exhausting and Katie felt she was losing momentum. Not to mention her mind.

The problem was she wasn't a naturally aggressive person, *normally*, and she was extremely hampered by the fact she knew she was behaving extremely badly. Nikos, on the other hand, obviously lacked any form of self-awareness; the man had autocratic leanings, which unless someone took him in hand soon would turn him into a fully fledged despot before long.

Nikos released a strangled expletive. 'It had not occurred to me,' he revealed coldly, 'that you would be stupid enough to lock the door.'

If he carries on talking to me as if I'm a silly child caught in misdemeanour I'll... She stopped mid furious thought as her mind produced an image to match his words.

'You mean if it hadn't been locked you'd have come barging in?' she yelped as a remarkably vivid image of Nikos exploding into the bathroom danced across her vision. For some reason her imagination had taken some poetic licence when it came to what he was wearing—*very little*! And as for having him leap energetically into the bath with her—that was a totally unnecessary sequel!

'If you were ill or in need of assistance, yes, I would have, but if you mean do I get my thrills from entering bathrooms uninvited? No, I do not.' Though his facial expression did not alter his abrupt shift of mood was evident in the smouldering gaze that rested on her face. 'If I get invited in...' he gave an expressive shrug '...that changes things.'

'The picture that conjures up makes me queasy.' For all

the wrong reasons, she thought. Jealousy was all she needed!

'I didn't realise that you had such prudish tendencies. Though I should have guessed when you said you and Tom do not talk about sex.'

'I am not a prude,' she denied angrily. Aware that her reaction was a bit OTT, she moderated her voice but couldn't prevent her distaste creeping in. 'I just think what goes on between a man and woman in private should remain that way and should not become the subject of crude jokes.'

'Well, at least you recognise it was a joke. Perhaps some food will help you gain some sense of proportion?'

If he wanted plain talking she'd show him she could do that too! 'And for your information we don't *talk* about sex, we *do* it!' She smiled triumphantly as she flaunted her non-existent sex life under his superior nose.

For a moment Nikos looked startled, then a deep laugh was wrenched from the depths of his throat. 'Thank you for sharing that with me,' he said solemnly.

Katie had never felt so humiliated in her life. She didn't know how she'd allowed herself to be goaded into making such a childish retort.

'Why shouldn't I have a healthy sex life? What's so funny about that?' she demanded.

'You talk about sex with the same swaggering bravado as a boy who has not yet lost his virginity.'

'I am not a boy.'

'Nor a v—'

'You know, I think I am a little hungry,' she cut in brightly.

This attempt to change the subject was so blatant that Nikos smiled. His smile guttered as an incredible thought occurred to him. He shook his head, dismissing it almost instantly; it was amazing what crazy ideas a man could get into his head when he hadn't eaten or slept.

Being an honest man, he couldn't be totally sure if his diminished mental acuity didn't lie at the door of a quite different basic need that was not being met. A basic need that he was conscious of every time he looked at his friend's lover…his own wife.

Nikos frowned. He had all the complications and surprises he needed in his business life; he made sure his personal life was unstressed and uncomplicated. It seemed if he wanted a return to that desirable status quo it would be necessary to remove Katerina Forsythe from his life as soon as possible. Which was the reason he'd come here, but somehow in between rescuing cats from burning buildings and being hospitalised he had been losing track of that detail.

'Fortunately I ordered enough for two in case you changed your mind.'

Katie looked beyond him and saw the glass-topped table set with a tempting array of light refreshments. Her stomach growled softly, reminding her of how little she'd eaten during the past twenty-four hours.

'Oh…' She gave a last wistful look at the spread. 'Actually I think I'm fine after all,' she explained unconvincingly.

'This sudden loss of appetite—is it a case of…cutting off your nose to spite your face? Have I got that right?' he asked innocently.

'Don't be cute!' she accused. 'Your English is a damned sight better than mine and we both know it,' she growled.

'Nobody has ever called me *cute* before. I'm touched.'

She found she couldn't carry on acting as though she were unaware of the malicious mockery in his lean face. 'So must I be…in the head!' She banged a hand against the side of the area in question. 'Just being here makes me certifiable.' Her expansive gesture took in the luxurious surroundings.

'Are you crying?'

Katie heard the wary quiver in his deep voice and remembered he didn't like women's tears.

'No, but it would serve you right if I was,' she told him, sniffing loudly.

Nikos's expression softened; she talked so tough but looked so vulnerable. The combination affected him strongly.

'It's true I don't like women's tears, but if anyone has reason to weep it is you. You have been very brave…but now you are tired and hungry. Come and eat. Let's call a truce.'

Though she was highly sceptical of his offer of a truce, quite irrationally his unexpected kindness cut through Katie's defences where all his clever taunts had not.

'What's on the sandwiches?' If she persisted in being stubborn, he might jump to the totally wrong conclusion—namely that she was scared to be in the same room as him!

Nikos had the good sense not to act as if he had won. 'Smoked salmon and cream cheese, beef and horseradish and cucumber?'

Katie found it hard not to drool. 'I am hungry.' As if to back up her words her stomach chose that moment to growl again—this time extremely loudly. Her glare dared him to laugh. 'And I hate to see good food go to waste.'

'Indeed,' he agreed, maintaining his gravity. 'Especially just to prove a point.'

'So much for a truce. I knew you couldn't do it!' she crowed.

'It doesn't start until we start eating.'

'Well, if you're going to make the rules up as we go along…'

'I surrender, you win,' he conceded, holding up his hands in mock submission.

'I'm not the one scoring points, I'm hungry.'

Nikos stepped aside to let her pass. 'So am I,' he murmured.

Katie took his enigmatic words at face value—she wasn't going somewhere that anybody with an ounce of sense would fear to tread!

Nikos led her to a long cream sofa piled high with plump cushions.

'Elevate your foot,' he suggested, pushing the cushions into a pile one end.

She had sat down at the opposite end before the extent of his inside knowledge struck her. 'How did you know I'm supposed to?'

Nikos slid a hand under her knees and neatly swivelled her round. 'I asked the doctor,' he divulged, placing her feet on the pile of cushions.

Katie's toes curled; she was astounded and indignant. 'And he told you?' So much for patient confidentiality.

'You are my wife.'

'Will you stop saying that?' she begged.

'Even if I do it will not change anything. I doubt the doctor saw any reason not to tell me. Now where is this bandage?'

'In my pocket.'

'It should be on your foot.'

'Well, I couldn't get it on, it's too tight. I tried.'

He held out his hand. 'Let me.'

Katie shook her head. 'Don't be silly.' She scooted her feet up the sofa and tucked them protectively under the hem of her robe.

A nerve began to pulse in his lean cheek. 'My touch offends you?'

'Don't be silly, of course not!' she scoffed.

Telling him what his touch actually did was naturally not an option.

'You are hyperventilating.'

'I am not and there really is no need for a bandage; my ankle feels perfectly fine after the bath.' Her voice rose to a shrill squeak in her frantic efforts to convince him.

'No, it is not, I saw you limping.'

Katie closed her eyes in frustration. 'Go on, have it your way,' she gritted, untucking her leg and stretching it out stiff-kneed.

She could hardly tell him the idea of him placing his hands on her skin for any length of time made her hot with excitement and cold with dread. What if she got turned on? Who was she kidding? There was no *if* about it! Hell, he only had to look at her and she felt emotionally mugged. What if when he touched her she did or said something *really* stupid?

Nikos silently looked at the ankle extended towards him but he made no attempt to touch it or her. The moment stretched on…

He remained motionless so long the muscles in her thigh started to quiver. The silence between them was heavy with tension; finally Katie could bear it no longer.

'Are you going to do this or not?' she demanded peevishly. *Not* would be good.

Nikos rolled up the sleeves of his shirt, revealing the sinewy strength of his forearms. Katie was engulfed by a wave of longing that filled her with despair.

'Then for goodness' sake get it over and done with!' she snapped.

When he did take her ankle between his big hands, they felt cool and capable. His attitude as he gently examined the tender bruised area was detached but sympathetic.

'It is badly swollen and the bruising is coming out.' His dark brows met in a frowning line as he examined her injury with strong, sensitive fingers. 'It looks extremely painful.'

It was, but this wasn't the reason Katie evaded his questioning glance. When she looked at him she saw his fingers touching, stroking areas on her body other than her ankle. The dangerous fantasy fuelled the pulse of inappropriate excitement that throbbed through her.

She took out her self-disgust on her innocent ankle. 'You didn't mention ugly,' she told him with a disconsolate sniff. With a frown she compared the injured ankle with her sound one; it was at least three times the size.

'I'm sure Tom will still love you if you had ankles as thick as tree trunks.'

She supposed it was the thought of Tom's uncritical adoration that brought the thin sneer to his lips. As far as Nikos was concerned she would never be good enough for his friend or him.

'I'm not so sure,' she mused half to herself as her thoughts turned to Tom's love of all things beautiful and perfect.

It was only his way of talking but sometimes, when Tom referred to her as his most precious possession, it made her uncomfortable. Tom liked his possessions in mint condition; if anything fell below the high standards he demanded he got rid of it. He had laughed and called Katie hopelessly sentimental when, after dropping a valuable vase, she hadn't let him throw it away.

'You bought it for me that day we went to an antique fair, and if I turn it like this,' she explained, 'you won't be able to see the crack at all.

'It's not worth anything now. I'll buy you another one.' He looked perplexed when she told him a new one wouldn't be the same.

'No, because then it won't have a flaw,' he replied drily.

Would he buy another wife just as easily when the old one got too worn? Katie was immediately ashamed of the unbidden thought.

'You place a high value on your looks and a low one on yourself.'

The stinging contempt in Nikos's voice brought Katie's attention swinging back to his face. She discovered he was angry. Inexplicably and impressively furious.

'If people can't see beyond your beautiful face and attractive figure, don't you see that that is their problem, not yours?'

Katie blinked in bewilderment at the harsh reproach in his voice. He thought she had a beautiful face…?

'I…' She bit back a cry of pain as his lean fingers tightened painfully around her bruised ankle.

Nikos immediately loosened his grip. 'I'm sorry I hurt you.'

'Not really,' she lied.

He grunted and slid her a look of irritation. Supporting her ankle against his own knee, he proceeded to roll the tubular bandage into a manageable shape.

'I would ask you to tell me if it hurts, but—' he raised his dark head from his task and there was an ironic gleam in his eyes '—I'd be wasting my time, wouldn't I?'

Katie doubted any pain could be worse than that sharp but sweet pleasure of having his fingers brush lightly against her skin.

'Thank you,' she said quietly when the support was back in place.

Nikos finished smoothing invisible wrinkles from the bandage over the curve of her calf and lifted his head; there was a faint flush along his high cheekbones. 'It was hardly brain surgery. Sit there,' he added. 'I'll bring you some food.'

'Oh! I thought I'd just take something to my room.'

One side of his mobile lips dropped. *'Running away?'*

'I can't run.'

'That's true. I don't like to eat alone; stay.'

Not likely. 'All right, I'll stay,' she heard herself reply. 'It seems a strange time of night to be eating.' But then it had been a strange day.

'You eat when you are hungry.'

Katie smiled at this simplistic philosophy; it was very Nikos.

'People have far too many hang-ups about food,' he revealed. 'How's this?' he added, passing her a laden plate.

'If I had any hang-ups about food I'd faint, but it looks great.' Her enthusiasm sounded false and hollow to her own ears; it was the fault of his slow-burning smile, the one that crinkled the corners of his eyes.

'We can pretend we're having a midnight feast, is that not what they do in English schools?'

'Not the one I went to,' Katie replied, thinking of the local comprehensive she had attended. She imagined it was a far cry from the sort of school Nikos had gone to. In fact her life was a far cry from his.

'Were you clever at school?'

'Not particularly,' she replied, suspicious of his interest. 'But I was very popular.' She gave a sudden impish grin that gave him a glimpse of the dry sense of humour that she had not had much opportunity to display in his company. 'But only because I had an extraordinarily handsome twin brother. You'd be amazed at how many girls wanted to come home for tea with me.'

'You were a twin?'

Katie, her mouth full of sandwich, nodded.

'It must have been especially hard for you to lose him,' he mused. Katie didn't reply; talking about Peter was still hard. 'What sort of man was your brother?'

Katie considered the question.

'He was handsome, impetuous, funny…' She stopped and flicked a wry look towards Nikos—best to beat him to the punchline. 'In short he was the exact opposite of me.'

He didn't dispute her assessment. 'You were the sensible twin?'

His perception was spooky; Peter had been the creative, impulsive twin and she had been the practical, grounded one.

'Peter was very special,' she said quietly.

'My brother was older, and we were not particularly

close. It was hard on my father when he died—Dimitri was his favourite.'

It was impossible to tell from his impassive expression whether he had minded this. Katie, seeing him as a little boy trying to gain parental approval, discovered that she had enough indignation for them both.

'He was groomed to take over virtually from birth. When we lost him my father literally almost worked himself to death because he didn't think I could fill my brother's shoes.'

And psychologists wondered why children went off the rails! With fathers around like the insensitive clot Nikos was describing it was a wonder any children ever turned out normal!

'That's so unfair!' she blurted out angrily. She flushed as he shot her a strange look. 'I just hope,' she added stiffly, 'I never make any child of mine feel inadequate,' she declared fiercely.

If Nikos had ever had any inadequacies he had obviously worked through them long ago—it was hard to imagine anyone *more* assured and confident than he was.

'And do you plan on having any children soon?'

Katie sighed. 'Tom doesn't think it would be a good idea to start a family for a few years yet.'

Nikos suspected she was unaware of how wistful she sounded. 'And you?' he probed gently.

'You shouldn't have a baby to fill a gap in your life.'

To Nikos it sounded as though she had told herself this many times before. 'Some people might say that if you are married to the right man you don't have a gap in your life.'

'Of course, but when you love someone it's only natural to want to have children with that person…' She looked at him, listening attentively to what she was saying, and stopped dead. 'I *am* marrying the right man!' He never lost an opportunity to get in a sly dig. *And how,* she wondered, *do I come to be babbling on like an agony aunt about life, love and babies with Nikos Lakis of all people?*

'Did I say otherwise? I was just making a general observation.'

'It didn't sound very general to me.' It was, she decided, her turn to ask the questions. 'This *father* of yours—' she couldn't keep the cold note of disapproval out of her voice '—does he pick out your bride too?' She knew that her mother's experience was not an isolated one, even now in the twenty-first century.

Nikos shook his head. 'My father says he's not giving me the excuse to turn around and say he's to blame when I mess up my marriage. His own marriage to my mother was arranged by their families; it was not a happy union,' he explained unemotionally. 'They virtually lived separate lives; when she died her lover phoned my father to tell him.'

Katie was unable to imagine living like that and what would it be like for the children of such a union?

'Cheer up.' He pressed a finger to the corners of her down-turned lips. 'He found true love the second time.'

His light touch had gone but the tingling sensation persisted. 'Poor true love,' she muttered mutinously.

Nikos looked amused by her venom. 'Oh, she manages to hold her own. You know, my father is not *all* bad. I have to admit in his defence that I did very little to disabuse him of the notion that I had no natural inclination for hard work. I was no angel.'

'Seven years married and now he tells me!'

His slow-burning smile appeared in response to her wry grin. It was almost, she mused, as if there was a connection, a real rapport between them; she froze, panic racing through her veins. *Connection! Rapport! You don't get cosy with the man who's doing his best to stop you marrying the man you love!*

'Listen,' she said with a tight smile that didn't reach her

worried eyes, 'you don't have to talk about your family with me.'

'Why—am I boring you?'

'No, you're not boring me.' Was he trying to be obtuse? 'It's a bit late for deep and meaningful discussions.' She yawned elaborately to emphasise her point.

'Isn't that what people do late at night?' he suggested softly. 'When the curtains are closed and the rest of the world does not exist. They reveal things about themselves that they would not dream of doing during the day. The night has a way of lowering barriers and thawing reserves.' His liquid dark gaze slid slowly over her body, then returned to her soft, trembling mouth. 'Of course,' he rasped throatily, 'they are usually in bed at the time and they do not spend all their time talking.'

Her sanity was history!

His voice was a sin!

She cleared her throat and tugged fretfully at the neck of her robe. It took all her will-power to wrench her lust-struck gaze from his face. At that moment she was extremely grateful that the towelling was so thick because her breasts were so tense and tender that in normal clothes the brazen changes in them would have been hard to miss.

'Well, we aren't…in bed!' she choked. 'That is, I don't want…you…we…' She closed her eyes and squared her shoulders. She could link more than two words together if she just put her mind to it and didn't look directly into his eyes.

'I'm sure I don't want to pry,' she announced, applying herself to the food even though her appetite had suddenly left her.

Considering his hunger, Nikos did not eat much, but he did watch her; in fact her appetite seemed to fascinate him. She tried not to let his interest put her off—it actually became a matter of principle not to let him see how much he spooked her, though she was beginning to suspect he already knew. He had to have seen the symptoms a hundred times before—he was the sort of man that women reacted to. In fact he probably took their homage as his due.

It occurred to her that he might be comparing her robust enjoyment of the food unfavourably with the more delicate, refined manners of his sophisticated lady friends.

'That was very nice, thank you.' Having started, Katie decided it seemed logical to get all the thank-yous out of the way at once. 'And thank you for saving my cat and giving me a bed tonight…it's kind of you,' she admitted primly.

Nikos looked at her with unsettling intensity for a moment. 'Perhaps you should try and get some sleep?' he suggested abruptly.

Katie nodded, unable to rid herself of the conviction he'd been about to say something quite different. Unable to endure his hard, steady appraisal any longer, she stood up. Aware of a strong and totally illogical feeling of anticlimax, she smoothed down the non-existent creases in her robe.

'I will.' Nikos's dark enigmatic eyes held hers but he still didn't speak. 'Goodnight?' Katie was deeply mortified to hear the word emerge as a wistful question. Her bare toes curled into the thick carpet. Could she be more obvious? She chastised herself, *Why don't you just go ahead and beg the man not to let you leave, Katie? That might be more subtle.*

'Goodnight, Katerina.'

Though his expression was about as revealing as a stone wall and his deep-accented drawl no more enlightening, Katie was totally convinced she read contempt in both. She limped towards the door before she could make any more of a fool of herself.

CHAPTER NINE

DESPITE the fact her body ached with exhaustion, Katie didn't find sleep quickly. Neither, it seemed, did Nikos—as she tossed she was aware of the crack of light under the door and maybe it was her overactive imagination but she seemed to hear his soft tread as he paced the room.

Eventually however she must have slept and when she awoke later in a cold sweat the light had gone and the room was in total darkness. She couldn't recall what she had been dreaming about, but when she had awoken whatever it was had left her with a nebulous sense of dread. In the unfamiliar surroundings it took her several clumsy attempts before she found the switch for the bedside light.

Despite the cluttered condition of her bedside table at home—the surface was crammed with framed snapshots of her family—she could locate the light switch with her eyes closed. In fact she frequently did.

A poignant smile curved her lips as her sleepy thoughts drifted to those well-loved family photos, none of which was going to win any prizes for composition or technique, but each one represented a precious memory for her… The one of Peter soaked to the skin but grinning after he'd taken a tumble into the pond they had picnicked beside. One of her favourites was her mother, who had believed herself unphotogenic, looking beautiful as she held aloft their birthday cake aflame with candles…*aflame*— The sound of the mental block in Katie's head crumbling was deafening.

'Oh, what am I going to do? They've all gone! Everything!' she cried out loud as the full horror of her loss came crashing down upon her.

The photos were gone…everything was gone. There was

nothing…not a single keepsake left of her mother, father or brother. She must have known this all along, but a protective mechanism had kicked in that had stopped her acknowledging it—until now.

Shoulders heaving, she turned over and buried her face in the pillow. Curled up in a tight foetal ball of misery beneath the duvet, Katie began to sob without restraint for what she had lost in the fire.

She was so immersed in this orgy of misery that she didn't hear the knock on the interconnecting door and she remained oblivious to the sound of a deep, concerned voice hesitantly calling her name. She wasn't even aware of the tall figure lowering himself down onto the edge of her bed. The hand on her shoulder was the first she knew of Nikos's presence.

'What's wrong?' He raked a hand through his tousled hair as he received a fresh wail in response. *'Speak to me!'* he demanded, shaking her slightly.

If Katie hadn't had other things on her mind she would have immediately noticed that his accent was perceptibly stronger and his air of calm command considerably frayed around the edges—but she did have other things on her mind.

Clutching the pillow her face was buried in even tighter with one hand, she used the other to hit out backwards. She didn't make contact.

'Nothing's wrong. Go away!' Her words emerged indistinctly through the pillow and the aching constriction in her throat.

'Clearly there is nothing wrong,' Nikos ironically observed. Eyes narrowed, he examined his options…then, giving vent to a harsh, guttural Greek curse, he flipped the hunched figure in the bed over onto her back. Katie didn't alter her position, she kept her knees folded up on her chest and her chin tucked into them.

'No doubt this cheery contentment is causing you to

weep as though your heart is broken,' he said drily as he proceeded to separate her from the pillow. 'You look like a baby hedgehog minus the spikes—on second thoughts, cancel the minus.'

Bereft of her protection, Katie covered her face with her arms, oblivious to how much of her naked state she revealed in the process. 'At least I have a heart!' she exclaimed. 'Will you just go away and leave me alone… *please*!' she added on an anguished note of entreaty as the sobs began to rise in her chest again.

Nikos drew a frustrated hand across a lean cheek, which was liberally sprinkled with an even layer of dark stubble. 'Do not be ridiculous, I cannot possibly leave you like this,' he told her grimly. 'Are you ill?'

'Go away!'

'Do you need a doctor? Is that it? I need to tell him what is wrong. Are you in pain? Does it hurt?'

'Only when I breathe.'

'Your chest hurts?'

'No.'

He released a tense sigh. 'I am going to call a doctor. I won't be long.'

Alarmed at the idea of medical intervention, she lifted an arm from her eyes and glared through jewel-bright, tear-filled eyes at him. 'Don't you *dare* call a doctor!' she snapped, emphasising her prohibition with a finger waved angrily in the general direction of his aristocratic nose.

'That,' Nikos approved, 'is better.' Almost casually he pinned her wrist against the pillow and then, after a very minor tussle, did the same with the other.

Katie's head thrashed angrily from side to side before she focused her wrath on the dark, demonically handsome face of the man looming over her. Her breath slowed and her expression grew unfocused. It was the first time she registered what he was wearing or, rather, *not*!

She had slept in the nude because she had no option;

Nikos obviously did so out of choice, because he clearly didn't have a stitch on beneath that robe. Which wouldn't have mattered so much if it had been a towelling hotel robe he was wearing, but this was a black silky thing that was knotted worryingly loosely about his waist as though he'd thrown it on in a hurry.

'What school of counselling did you attend?' she asked hoarsely.

'Talk to me,' Nikos replied with the air of someone who was not going to be easily distracted from his purpose.

Katie envied his focus; her own couldn't even withstand the warm, uniquely male fragrance rising from his body. To her dismay when he leaned forward to cause the revealing robe to gape even more, exposing in the process most of his chest and a great deal of his flat belly, and if she hadn't stopped herself looking—it hadn't been easy—probably even more.

'Why should I?' she demanded, reasserting control over her wandering eyes. It might be different if he actually cared, she thought dully, and why should he? *First I'm an inconvenient wife he preferred to pretend didn't exist, now I'm an embarrassingly emotionally incontinent guest.* By now he must be wishing he hadn't taken pity on her homeless condition.

'Because you want me to go away, and I won't do so until you have,' he explained simply.

'What,' she asked facetiously, 'do you want me to talk about? The weather?'

Nikos was pleased to recall an annoying phrase that Caitlin was inordinately fond of using. It seemed appropriate for the occasion.

'It is not good to keep things bottled up.'

Katie was so astonished to hear this advice emerging from his mouth that she stopped struggling. '*You're* giving *me* advice on expressing emotions?' She blinked. 'You're priceless, you really are.'

Nikos decided to try another tack.

'What' he asked with a dizzying change of subject, 'are you wearing?'

Katie froze and tried to slide a little farther under the duvet. 'What's that got to do with anything?'

He lifted one brow and smiled blandly. 'Not a thing, but I was just thinking how easy it would be to find out, if I were a man totally without scruples.'

Katie ran the tip of her tongue over the outline of her dry lips and swallowed. 'Are you trying to blackmail me?' she squeaked as she considered her options. He was almost certainly bluffing, but could she risk it? 'Let me go. *Please...*'

Nikos's dark glance dwelt thoughtfully on her face for several seconds and then with a slight inclination of his head he released her wrists.

With a white-knuckled grip on the duvet, Katie slithered a little farther upright, raising the cover to her chin as she did so.

'I was crying because I have lost everything in the fire.'

'Were you not insured?'

Katie threw him a scornful look. 'I'm not talking about things with monetary value; I don't care about them!' she declared with a disdainful sniff.

Nikos's gaze narrowed as he listened to the woman who had married a stranger for money contemptuously dismiss her possessions. Nikos did not like anomalies.

'Some things can't be replaced with a cheque.' She caught her lower lip between her teeth to stop it trembling. 'All the photos of my parents and brother...all the keepsakes... Mum kept the oddest things—a curl from our first haircut, Peter's certificate when he won first prize in the fancy dress competition, the theatre programme from her first proper date with Dad.'

With a cry she rolled onto her side and pressed her hand

over her mouth. Nikos went to touch her but her slim body tensed in rejection and with a twisted smile he drew back.

'They all went up in the fire,' she explained dully, when she had composed herself. She rolled onto her back. 'There's nothing left!' she told him in a tight, controlled voice that couldn't disguise the bleakness in her eyes. Despite her attempt to stay in control, her voice rose as her anguish-filled eyes locked angrily with his.

At one level she knew that it was unfair to make him a target of her anger, but her anger didn't listen to reason, it just needed an outlet.

'Does that constitute just cause in your eyes? I suppose you think I'm being hopelessly sentimental crying about things most people would throw away?' she goaded.

Feeling herself losing control—or was it the emotion she saw in his eyes she couldn't take?—she lowered her eyes to her fingers, which were restlessly picking at the edge of the cotton cover.

'It is just cause, and, as for sentimentality, that is not a crime in my homeland. We Greeks are a sentimental race.'

Katie lifted her head jerkily and looked with astonishment at the grave expression on his face. Would this man ever stop surprising her? she wondered. Every time she thought she had a handle on him he did something that made her retrench.

'But I think you are wrong—you have not lost everything.'

Katie's anger stirred. He'd been in there, he must know that nothing had survived. It was cruel of him to try and raise false hopes just to save himself the discomfort of her tears!

'The fire may have burned paper and twisted metal beyond recognition but some things were beyond its reach…' He reached over and touched the side of her head with his forefinger. 'Inside here you have the memories of a lifetime and nothing can ever rob you of those,' he told her softly.

Her eyes shot to his and what she saw there convinced her of his total sincerity. He was not just mouthing empty platitudes, he believed totally in what he had just said.

'Oh!' she breathed, moved to tears by what he had said, but this time they were tears of appreciation not despair. He was right—some things nobody could take away from her. She could keep her memories, treasure and polish them. She lifted her hand to dab the moisture leaking from her eyes and felt the duvet slip; she immediately grabbed it again.

Nikos folded his arms across his chest and watched her contortions. 'Let me?'

Before she could voice a protest he lifted his hand and blotted the salty moisture from her cheek with his thumb. Her body's response to the soft touch was immediate and devastating. The devastation was not confined to the area of her downy cheek he stroked; her entire body was filled with a heavy, throbbing lassitude. Katie's eyelashes brushed her cheek as they flickered weakly downwards.

'There's really no need,' she murmured vaguely.

Nikos looked down into the upturned face of the young woman beside him, his dark eyes touching the blue-veined tracery on her flickering eyelids, the faint, tell-tale flush of blood beneath her pale skin, the vulnerable exposed line of her lovely throat and the pulse spot that throbbed at the base of that throat.

He was barely touching her and she was aroused. The natural progression of his male thoughts led him to visualise how she might respond if he did more than stroke her cheek…such a soft cheek, such smooth skin. Was it equally smooth all over? His heated glance dropped from her lush lips to her smooth, bare shoulders…

'No,' he agreed throatily. 'No need at all.' The statement was noticeably lacking in his usual absolute conviction.

Katie sighed low in her throat, an almost feline sound of

pleasure, and turned her head so that the circular movement of his thumb now moved over an area as yet untouched.

The action caused a section of her long silky hair to fall across her cheek. Nikos brushed it aside, but instead of removing his hand he slid his fingers deep into the thick glossy mass until they could trace the shape of her skull.

Katie gave a voluptuous sigh of pleasure.

'I should go,' he said throatily.

Katie's eyes shot open in protest. *'You can't!'* She encountered the sensual heat of his smouldering eyes and her heart started to slam against her ribs. She moistened her lips with the tip of her tongue and swallowed. 'You could stay?'

Nikos inhaled sharply, the action sucking in his flat belly and swelling his magnificent bronzed chest. His eyes slid from hers, his lush lashes effectively concealing his expression; this didn't stop Katie imagining the embarrassed distaste no doubt mirrored there. Her misery was complete when he turned his head away and expelled his suspended breath with a low, sibilant hiss.

No wonder he can't look at me. Self-respect, pride… remember what those are, Katie?

'No, of course not, that's a silly idea. Take no notice of me, I'm in shock…yes, that's it, I'm in shock!' she heard herself cry in manic relief. 'Let's just forget I said it. I didn't mean it.'

Nikos spun back to her, his eyes blazing. 'Yes, you did!' he contradicted rawly. 'And *I can't forget*!' The explosive pronouncement seemed to be ripped from his throat.

Katie swallowed, mesmerised by the lambent glow in his silvered eyes. 'Why not…?'

'Because,' he said in the manner of someone making an uncomfortable discovery, 'I don't want to.'

Katie gasped as a pleasure-pain knifed through her body.

Sexual longing of a type she hadn't known existed made her bold; it also made her reckless and single-minded. Her tunnel vision saw no consequences, only need—a need that consumed her. Every fibre of her being was mindlessly intent on assuaging the hunger, which no part of her was free of.

'What *do* you want?' she whispered, wondering how much more of this torment she could take.

Her desire for him went bone-deep; she wanted the taste of him, the feel of him, she wanted all of him… She'd never experienced anything like this before and had no defences against it.

'The same thing I've wanted to do since the first moment I met you…' Arms braced either side of her shoulders, he lowered himself with a beautifully fluid movement down until she could feel his warm breath shiver against her skin. He adjusted the angle of his head so his lips were positioned directly over hers and their warm breaths mingled.

Anticipation of his kiss made her dizzy, but despite the tension that every taut line of his body screamed Nikos was in no hurry.

'Your mouth is truly edible,' he rasped smokily as, holding her eyes with his, he took tiny soft bites almost too light for her to feel from the quivering outline.

The sexy rumble of his voice made her tremble. Through the fluttering shield of her lowered lashes she studied his rampantly male features, dizzy with anticipation.

'No!' He shook his head very slightly as her heavy eyelids closed. 'I want you to look at me.'

Katie responded to his instruction without thinking, though her eyelids felt as though they were weighed down. 'I was looking at you, I can't seem to help myself,' she said, not trying to evade his searching eyes. 'What else do you want me to do?'

'I want you to open your mouth for me.'

'I want that too,' she revealed, gazing up at him with unconcealed desire. *'I want you,'* she added simply in a voice that literally *ached* with longing, silently adding that this was what she'd wanted for seven long years.

A hot flood of hoarse words spilled from Nikos as his darkened eyes sealed to hers; he seemed completely unaware that he had spoken in Greek. Katie barely registered it herself. The only thing she needed to understand was in his smoky eyes and they said the same thing in any language—he wanted her! And she wanted him—oh, how she wanted him!

Why didn't I know that surrender felt this sweet, this empowering? Katie thought dreamily. The satisfaction didn't come solely from surrendering to him, it was from surrendering to her own passion.

He rolled onto his side and, with one big hand supporting the back of her head, took her with him, all the while pressing hot, frantic kisses to her face and neck as throaty words of Greek and English spilled from his lips.

The fine tremors afflicting her entire body became deep shudders as he finally fitted his mouth to hers.

Katie whimpered at the expert pressure of his lips, the whimper became a fierce groan as his clever tongue stabbed smoothly deep into the sweet warmth of her mouth and then again and again...parodying a more intimate invasion.

Through the thickness of the duvet Katie curved her pliant body into his muscular frame and even though several inches of duck down separated them she could feel the urgency of his arousal. She took hold of his head between her hands and, meshing her fingers deep in his rich, luxuriant hair, she met his tongue tentatively with her own—then again, more boldly.

If this was depravity she wanted more of it—she never wanted to break the contact; she wanted it to go on for ever and ever.

Nikos continued to kiss her with the same blind, driving urgency as he smoothly rolled her underneath him. He performed the move with the same fluid grace he did everything, but at that moment she was willing to forgive him for being perfect. Very few things Katie had experienced had ever felt as incredibly marvellous as the weight of his warm, hard body pinning her to the bed. The intimate pressure of his erection grinding into her soft belly made her whimper softly into his mouth.

Panting, they finally broke apart like divers breaking to the surface in search of oxygen. Nikos rolled away to one side, his chest heaving; he lifted his arm across his face, wiping the sheen of sweat from his brow. It remained there, concealing his expression from her.

Eyes glazed and glittering, face flushed, Katie reached for him; actually she couldn't bear *not* to touch him. His body was incredible; every detail of it held a fascination for her. She had enough oxygen stored up to last at least another two kisses and she shook with the need to get out of her depth again—and fast!

'You've wanted to do that all night?' she asked wonderingly as she stroked his arm. His flesh had a deliciously silky texture and the toned muscles were hard and compact and beautifully formed beneath her fingertips. She'd had her suspicions, but it came as some relief to have it confirmed that her lustful fantasies had not been one-sided.

'I've wanted to do that since seven years ago,' he corrected huskily.

Katie's eyes widened. 'I had no idea I made such an impact.'

'Impact!' he echoed, releasing a strange, strangled laugh. 'I think you could safely say you did that, Katerina. When I walked into that cheap, nasty little room I expected...' Katie saw the muscles of his strong brown throat work as he swallowed.

'A cheap and nasty bride?' she suggested sadly. Only her loyalty to the memory of her brother stopped her explaining there and then why she had taken the drastic decision to buy a bridegroom.

'Well, let's just say I wasn't expecting a girl who looked like a sexy kitten. All enormous, trusting blue eyes, a sexy mouth and a cloud of the most incredible silky hair. It put me in a vile temper to realise I was as weak as any other man; I had considered I was immune to such things.'

He had known of course that she couldn't have been the wide-eyed innocent she'd appeared, which in his considered opinion had made her all the more dangerous. But he had begun to wonder if he shouldn't have followed his gut instincts in this instance and to hell with consequences. He had a strong suspicion that his gut instincts might have been closer to the truth than the judgment he'd made based on more practical considerations.

'Add to that you looked about sixteen.'

'I was eighteen,' she corrected him huskily.

'And you had—correction, *have*—a body that could make a grown man weep.'

A sound halfway between a groan and a laugh was wrenched from his chest as his arm lifted from his face revealing a rigid mask of constraint. As he scanned her face some of his control slipped, offering her a glimpse of a raw hunger that made her stomach muscles clench violently.

'I know that marriages nowadays are not noted for their durability, but how many men who meet the most beautiful and desirable woman they have ever seen marry her then walk away swearing not to remain faithful, but never to see or contact her again?'

He lifted a section of her silky hair and let it slip through his fingers. 'You know, *yineka mou*, I think we have some unfinished business.'

Katie nodded. 'I nearly asked Harvey about you,' she admitted shyly. 'But I couldn't, not after making such a fuss about wanting there to be no contact.'

'Do you still not desire contact?' His low, seductive drawl sent a stab of white-hot sexual desire through her body.

She shook her head and urgently moaned his name. In

her naivety she'd expected his kisses to ease her hunger, but instead they had acted as a release valve for all the pent-up sensuality that had been dammed up inside her for years. Her passionate nature had found a focus—Nikos.

'So sweet, so wild.'

His husky appreciation jolted her. *He thinks I'm going to be good at this. He's expecting a sex goddess—heavens, does he have it all wrong!* Telling him she was a virgin would be just too mortifying; there had to be some other way to explain her lack of competence…?

'No!' she denied, twisting to evade his lips. 'I'm not wild—in fact I'm not a sexy sort of person,' she blurted out.

Her revelation did not have any immediate effect; Nikos carried on kissing her neck with just as much dedication as before. Katie's concentration drifted as she felt the resistance slip from her body. 'Did you hear what I said, Nikos?' She hoped so because she couldn't say it again.

Nikos gave her neck a nibble before raising his head. 'You have my full attention. So you are not sexy?' Laughter formed in his liquid dark eyes and his lips twitched. Even with his hair tousled he looked incredibly gorgeous.

Katie observed with dismay that he didn't seem to be taking her very seriously. 'Ask Tom if you don't believe me.' As wrong things to say went, this was right up there in the top three.

She wasn't exactly surprised when Nikos's expression froze over. 'I don't require references from your lovers.'

Lovers! Gracious, he was really missing the point—it being she hadn't had any of the above and he'd had dozens…hundreds probably! Therein lay the problem.

'And I forbid you to *think* about Tom.' His powerful body curved over hers. 'Do you hear me?'

'I hear you, Nikos!' she said, awed and even—quite shockingly—a little turned on by his masterful behaviour.

Nikos scanned her face; whatever he saw there must have satisfied him because then he nodded before he kissed her again, long, deep, drugged kisses that left her craving more.

Katie gave a soft moan as he left her mouth to lick and bite his way down her throat until he reached the wildly throbbing pulse spot at the base of her neck. His breath, which came in uneven gasps, was hot against her bare skin.

'I want to see you,' he informed her in a thickened voice that was not entirely steady.

At his words a white-hot flame of desire pulsed through her throbbing body like a blade. Along with it came a thread of doubt…which she firmly squashed.

Katie had never craved a man's approval before. Taking her courage by the scruff of the neck, she pushed away the mesh of hair that had fallen across her face. Looking directly into his eyes, she peeled back the quilt in one quick motion.

Nikos inhaled sharply. Katie's self-doubt began to flow steadily away from her as he examined her body in an almost reverent silence. A primitive mask of need tautened his lean features as his liquid dark eyes consumed her with the single-minded concentration of a starving man confronted with a feast.

'So pale, so perfect. You are beautiful, *yineka mou*,' he asserted shakily. 'Just looking at you makes me burn.'

Katie ran a finger across his cheek feeling drunk with her newly discovered feminine power. That she could excite such feelings in a man like this…why, nothing seemed impossible now.

'You make me feel very strange,' she confided innocently.

The not-so-innocent sultry smile that accompanied her words provoked an immediate response from Nikos. He laughed huskily and framed her flushed face with his hands. Her pulse gave a lustful surge as she stared in awed wonder at the thrillingly primitive expression etched on his strong-boned, beautiful face.

'You make me feel very hot,' he revealed with a wolfish grin that made her quiver inside and out.

She watched, not daring to breathe, her heart thumping like a wild thing as he curled his hand around the swell of her breast. A voluptuous sigh of pleasure escaped from between her clenched teeth; his touch on her bare skin was electric.

The expression on his face as he traced the tip-tilted profile of first one breast and then the other with his expert fingers was rapt. When his eyes lifted to hers there was a raw, needy look on his face that made her insides dissolve.

His exploration homed in on her nipple; she stopped breathing as he took the prominent bud between his thumb and forefinger, and the resulting friction made her body arch.

'Good?'

Katie opened her eyes. 'Very good. Do it again!' she demanded.

He did.

Lips parted, eyes shut tight, she squirmed restlessly as his thumb moved back and forth across the rosily engorged nipple at the centre. He ran his tongue over the sensitised flesh and sensual overload sent Katie's head backwards into the pillow.

She had barely assimilated the sensual delights of this sensation when his exploration moved lower. His skilful fingers left a burning trail as they skimmed lightly over her belly. As his exploration boldly widened to include the soft fuzz of hair at the apex of her legs Katie found she could hardly breathe for the intense excitement that held her in its vicelike grip.

With sultry abandon she looked up at him through half-closed eyes. The mindless hunger she felt was reflected in the stark mask of need that contorted his dark features. She caught her tongue between her teeth and gasped as, with his eyes melded to hers, he allowed his fingers to slide between her legs into the slick heat of her aching core.

Katie moaned and felt the heat spread across her lower abdomen. Eyes locked to his, she parted her long legs in wanton invitation. With a muttered imprecation Nikos loosened the belt of his robe in a frenzied manner.

'My God, but you have a beautiful body!'

Shooting her a quick, predatory grin, he continued.

Simply looking at his sleek, streamlined, rampantly male body brought an emotional ache to her throat that had nothing to do with simple lust—she wasn't actually surprised, she supposed that deep down she'd always known the feelings he aroused were more complex…more dangerous.

He finally shed his black silky robe, revealing to her mesmerised gaze a fully aroused male in all his glory. 'Oh, my!' she gasped shakily as he rejoined her on the bed.

'Touch me!' he invited, kissing her lips. 'Don't you want to?'

'Oh, yes!' She touched his collar-bone; it was very nice, but there were other areas that interested her more.

Nikos seemed to share her view because, smiling into her eyes, he took her hand and fed it onto a more enticing area of his body. She felt the fine muscles under the smooth skin of the surface of his belly contract violently—she was hooked!

Katie released a long, shuddering breath and, no longer tentative, trailed her fingers over his warm brown flesh, making return journeys to areas that seemed particularly sensitive. The texture of his flesh was incredible; she wanted to taste it.

What's stopping you?

With growing confidence in her ability to excite him, she let her lips and tongue follow the pathway her fingers had previously traced down his tense, quivering body.

Nikos lay, his eyes half closed, accepting her ministrations until her exploration got bolder.

Lying on her back, her arms pinned either side of her head, she was about to protest but he got in first.

'My turn, I think,' he said, slipping down her body.

He seemed to know exactly where, how and for how long to touch her in order to send her out of control and keep her there. Katie didn't want to think how he'd got so good at what he was doing to her, she just wanted to enjoy it, and she did.

'I can't take any more of this,' she gasped weakly, when he eventually returned to her mouth.

'Just a little more…' he promised, settling between her thighs. His face a mask of rigid restraint, he slid into her with one smooth thrust.

A fractured gasp hissed through her clenched teeth at the sharp pain, but then it was gone and he was still there filling her, stretching her in a wonderful way that she could not have imagined. Experimentally she moved; this was when she realised that Nikos was not moving. He was dead still.

She opened her eyes to find him watching her with an expression of white-faced incredulity; his body was quivering with the effort of not moving.

'There's more?'

Katie felt the sound of hoarse amusement that was wrenched from his throat. 'Let me show you, *yineka mou*.'

Her throaty, *Please,* was lost inside his mouth but her awed, 'That is incredible,' to inadequately describe the sensation of him moving inside her was clearly audible. Pretty soon after that she lost all ability to say anything coherent, though when she felt his hot release pulse into her body a couple of seconds after she'd been blown away by a shattering climax she did manage to speak, but only the one word.

'Nikos!'

It was amazing how much feeling and variation a person

could put into two syllables, especially if you said them over and over and over again!

Once she could speak it seemed better to anticipate any awkward cross-examination.

'Before you ask, yes, I was. But,' she added with a languid smile, 'if I'd known it could be like that I wouldn't have been.' This out of the way, she curled up like a kitten in his arms and went to sleep.

CHAPTER TEN

KATIE woke to the smell of coffee. Eyes closed, she stirred, drowsily conscious that something was subtly different. She tried to focus her thoughts but the extra ingredient remained tantalisingly out of reach. It was several sleepy minutes later when it hit her with the dramatic impact of a force ten hurricane; she gasped and stilled.

Oh, no, it's me, I'm different. Beautifully different. I slept with Nikos Lakis.

A wondering smile drew the corners of her mouth upwards. Rolling onto her side, she reached out. Her smile faded when she discovered only a sheet, its crumpled condition standing a silent accusing testament to the vigour of their lovemaking through the night.

She closed her eyes as a jumbled kaleidoscope of the events of the night slid across her inner vision. What she saw shocked and excited her; it also provided an explanation for the unaccustomed tenderness in several parts of her body.

The only cloud on her horizon was Tom—she had to tell him. She felt ashamed that she had treated him so badly, but she'd always known in her heart that they weren't right for each other. She knew that Tom did too. Not that she had any excuse.

'You are awake?'

Katie's head whipped around, her face bright with expectation and excitement she could not hide.

Nikos was standing at the bedside, a towel wrapped around his narrow hips. The wet hair plastered to his skull and the drops of water still clinging to his shoulders indicated he had just stepped from the shower.

'You shouldn't have let me sleep,' she told him shyly.

'You needed the sleep,' he replied without meeting her eyes.

'I slept as much as you did.' The memory of what they had done instead of sleeping brought a rush of warmth to her cheeks.

'I don't need much sleep,' he replied flatly.

Katie was finding it increasingly difficult to conceal her growing consternation. *Well, what did you expect—that he wouldn't be able to keep his hands off you?* She released a rueful sigh; well, actually yes, she had, but what did she know about the way people behaved the morning after?

Maybe Nikos wasn't a morning person, but in her eyes he more than compensated by being a night-time person.

Her eyes flickered hungrily along his lean, streamlined body; the moisture on his brown skin emphasised the rippling muscles of his spare torso and delineated each individual muscle in his washboard-flat belly.

At the sight of him her doubts dissolved before they had fully formed. What was to regret? Last night had been the most incredible experience of her life. Nikos was the perfect lover and just looking at him made her ache. Her eyes darkened as she recalled waking in the night to find him looking at her. Neither of them had spoken, they hadn't needed words; he had come to her and she'd been ready for him. Just thinking about the urgent primal coupling made her breasts swell and tingle.

Her breath came quickly as she half closed her eyes and imagined touching him, running her hands over the hard contours of shoulders and chest, tangling her fingers in the soft whorls of dark hair that lay against the brown skin there. The heat inside her grew as she gloatingly anticipated running her fingertips over the damp hairs on his muscular flanks and feeling his stomach muscles quiver beneath her flattened palms as she laid them against his flat belly.

She'd save the best until last.

The sexual heat coiled in her belly spilled through her entire body in response to the tactile imagery of holding his silky hard length in her hand…she released a hoarse sigh and lifted her shaken gaze to his.

Their eyes touched and Katie could almost taste the passion flare between them; she felt the electrical current of mutual attraction crackle and spark.

Then as if a switch had been flicked it was gone. Nikos's expression was—actually it wasn't so much what was there that made her feel uneasy, it was what wasn't there.

This couldn't be right.

She smiled questioningly up at him, and got nothing back in response, not even a hint as to what was going on behind those shuttered eyes. Despite this Katie felt an incredible swell of love in her chest as she looked at him. The outpouring of emotion was so intense that she could hardly breathe.

She was seized with an irrational desire to share with him how much the previous night had meant to her. She had to bite her tongue to stop herself blurting out something stupid.

'That coffee smells good.'

'I'll get you some.' A muscle flexed along his strong, angular jaw.

Katie viewed this development with considerable dismay. *Maybe he's regretting last night.*

'Did the phone wake you?'

She shook her head. 'I don't think so.' She took a resolute breath and steeled herself to hear something she didn't want to. 'Nikos, what's wrong? Have I done something?'

His eyes swept over her face. 'You were perfect!' he declared fiercely.

Katie didn't want to be perfect, she wanted to be loved, or failing that at least *wanted.* Being wanted by Nikos would be better than being loved by any other man.

'Then why—?' she began.

Before she could finish there was a knock on the door. Housekeeping bringing a fresh change of towels, no doubt. Katie would have let them go away, but Nikos called out for them to come in.

With a grunt of frustration Katie pulled the quilt up to her chin. Her mood lightened considerably when, after dropping his towel, Nikos slid into the bed beside her.

With a sigh she insinuated her soft curves up against him, revelling in the strength of his lean body. His body felt cool against her warm skin. Without saying anything he pulled her almost savagely into his arms. Holding her eyes, he brushed his mouth against hers in a tentative, questioning way. She trembled.

'This is wrong!'

'It feels pretty right to me.' She tried to keep the rising panic from her voice.

'Katerina?' he began urgently.

Katie pressed a finger to his lips. 'I know what you're going to say.'

'You do?'

Katie nodded. 'And I feel badly about Tom too, but it wasn't something we planned.'

'Katerina...'

'Don't talk, not now,' she begged huskily.

With a groan he crushed her to him. His kiss was bruising and had an element of desperation about it. Katie felt something equally primitive inside her stir and respond to the demands of his lips and tongue.

Breathing hard, she rested her forehead against his chin, shivering as his hands closed tight across her back, pressing her sensitised breasts up against his chest.

'Nikos, would you really hate it if I fell in love with you?'

Nikos went white and flinched as though she'd struck him. Katie knew immediately that something had gone badly wrong; it wasn't until ten seconds later that she knew just how badly!

'Oh, my God!'

Katie turned and saw a white-faced Tom standing there in the bedroom, staring at them as though his world had just come to an end.

'Tom?' Icy shock, bitter regret, guilt that she was responsible for putting that look of disillusionment on his face hit Katie simultaneously. 'Oh, Tom, I'm so sorry,' she whispered. 'So very sorry.'

Tom didn't reply, he just turned on his heel and walked unsteadily away.

Katie lay there, her hand pressed to her lips, her eyes tight shut, but even with her eyes tight shut she could see Tom's face, see the bleak disillusionment she had put there. Suddenly she sat up and, running a shaking hand through her disordered hair, swung her legs over the side of the bed.

'I have to go to him!' she gritted in some agitation.

'I doubt very much if he wants to see you,' Nikos rasped drily.

Turning to him in protest, Katie was shocked to see the grey, unhealthy tinge to his skin and the grim and bleak light in his heavy-lidded eyes. Of course Nikos must feel every bit as wretched as she did; Tom was his friend. Katie felt a fresh spasm of guilt, this time because she'd been too busy thinking abut how she felt to consider how bad this was for Nikos.

She brought her knees up to her chin and wrapped her arms around them.

'Perhaps later?'

Nikos laughed; it wasn't a pleasant sound. 'Think again,' he advised. 'The man just found you in bed with his friend,' he reminded her brutally.

Katie flinched and buried her face in her hands. 'I wouldn't have had him find out like this for the world!'

Telling him was always going to be a messy, unpleasant business, but this had been awful.

'Perhaps it is for the best this way.'

She rubbed her temples where the pressure had reached critical level. 'I don't see how. What I don't understand is how he knew I was here?'

'He heard about the fire on the local radio station and he rang me to ask if I had any idea where you'd stayed last night.'

Katie shook her head to clear the fog that was making her thought processes slow and stupid. 'He rang you?' she parroted.

'From the lobby,' Nikos confirmed. 'I told him to come on up.'

'You told him, I don't understand...' Suddenly Katie felt cold inside, icy cold and empty. 'But why?' she faltered, seeking an explanation for the inexplicable cruelty in his actions. 'Why would you do that?'

'Tom deserves to know that you don't love him.'

'Of course he does, but not like this...it's not as if I was going to stay with him...I couldn't. I mean, you can't think that I'd have gone through with the marriage after last night? Oh, no,' she gasped. 'You did, didn't you?' Still he didn't reply.

His silence was a reply.

'You set me up!' She said it, but part of her still couldn't quite believe it. How could anyone make love the way he had when all the time they were planning to...? A choked sound of distress emerged from between her clenched teeth.

Nikos started forward and then stopped, his nostrils flaring as she shrank back from him, her expression one of loathing. 'You should lie down.'

She rained contemptuous eyes to his face. 'Oh, you're so considerate,' she snarled.

'I didn't plan this,' he told her heavily. 'You have to believe that I only—'

'I have to believe absolutely *nothing* you say,' she corrected him coldly. 'I suppose you *accidentally* directed Tom in here and you just didn't stage that kiss for his benefit either?' She wiped a shaking hand roughly across her mouth.

Nikos's jaw tightened. 'I couldn't be sure you wouldn't go back to him. I could not permit that.'

What a cheek, he didn't even try and deny it any more. 'I suppose you're proud of what you've done? I suppose this constitutes true friendship for someone as emotionally stunted as you,' she observed bleakly. 'You sleep with a woman you despise to save your friend from her evil clutches and you think that's what a true friend does?'

Hand pressed to her mouth, she ran to the bathroom where she was violently sick.

Grabbing hold of the washbasin, she heaved herself upright. Her legs shook and her skin felt clammy.

She looked at the wet flannel Nikos held out to her and laughed. *'You have to be joking...?'*

Face white as chalk, her expression one of proud disdain, she walked past him, chin held high.

'If you don't mind I'd like a bath—to wash you off my skin.' From the corner of her eyes she caught her reflection in a mirror and registered her naked state for the first time. 'And I need clothes...' she added vaguely.

She turned on a tap and turned back, her cold mask cracking to reveal the aching anguish beneath. 'Did you plan this all along...you planned all along to seduce me?' She could no longer say made love. 'Silly question, of course you did...you planned it down to the last detail.'

'Including the fire?'

'I wouldn't put anything past you!' she declared, glaring at him in simmering distaste. 'But I suppose the fire just made things easier.' *And I was very easy,* she thought bitterly.

'If you had truly loved Tom you would not have been

in my bed last night. If you had had any sort of relationship you would not have come to my bed a virgin.'

'Tom respects me!' she declared furiously. 'Not that you'd know anything about that.'

'You're right there, I wouldn't. Perhaps if Tom hadn't respected you so much,' he sneered, 'you wouldn't have fallen into my bed so readily last night.'

The sound of her hand connecting with his lean cheek resounded shockingly around the room.

'Face it, Katerina, your whole relationship with Tom was a lie. What were you expecting to happen when the ring was on your finger? That passion would suddenly ignite, or were you prepared to sacrifice love for security and money?' he wondered contemptuously.

'You can try and deflect the guilt as much as you like, Nikos, but we both know that you behaved like a rat.'

'I didn't force you to do anything you didn't want to do last night,' he told her quietly. 'And I didn't suggest anything you haven't been thinking of from the first moment we met again.' His burning eyes travelled over the heaving contours of her breasts before dropping to her belly...beads of sweat appeared across his upper lip when he reached the soft dark fuzz between her thighs. 'And we both know that even now if I touched you you'd be begging me to take you,' he declared arrogantly.

'I hate you,' she whispered.

'For telling the truth? If you care so much for the luxuries money can buy, I am far richer than Tom.'

Katie felt a flash of blind rage. 'You think you can buy me?' she quivered.

'Do not be dramatic, that is not what I am saying.' Nikos strove to retain his calm in the face of her determination to misread everything he said. 'I am simply pointing out that lack of funds is not an issue, I am able to provide for you and unlike Tom I have no problem with you working.'

Was he for real? 'My, isn't that big of you?' she drawled.

Nikos felt his control slip. 'Perhaps we should discuss this later when you are able to speak rationally,' he gritted.

'I want to talk now and there isn't going to be any later for you and I, not without a lawyer present anyhow. Let me get this straight—are you asking me to be your mistress?'

'You are my wife.'

Katie laughed. 'Not for very much longer. Sleep with you! I can't bear to be in the same room as you!' she told him in a throbbing voice.

His dark eyes snapped. 'If I go now it will be for good,' he warned her.

'At last,' she sighed. 'Light at the end of the tunnel.'

'You will miss me every day for the rest of your life, Katerina!' Nikos predicted as he turned on his heel and left.

Katie heard the door slam. The awful part was he was probably right; she was a one-man woman, it was just her luck that that man happened to be an untrustworthy bastard!

CHAPTER ELEVEN

'THERE'S someone asking to see you, Katie,' Georgina hissed as she poked her head around the door. 'And she looks like *pure money*,' she added.

'Does this money have a name?' Katie asked, trying to inject a note of animation into her flat voice.

Despite the black cloud of despondency that had positioned itself above her head, she really did make a determined effort to appear her normal cheerful self at work. Nobody liked to be around a misery guts.

'It's CJ Malone,' the older woman twittered excitedly. 'You know, the fashion designer.'

'I know,' said Katie, thinking of the blue dress.

'Actually it's Caitlin Lakis; Malone was my maiden name.' The tall figure who strode calmly into the room approached Katie's desk, hand confidently outstretched.

Katie got to her feet, all the colour leeching from her face. 'Kyria Lakis.' She used the title even though she knew, because the relevant papers that would free Nikos to marry were at that very moment in her bag, this couldn't be strictly accurate.

As the woman who was trying the name on for size—you couldn't miss, it fitted her like a glove—seemed to be studying her with frank, but not unfriendly curiosity, Katie thought it legitimate to return that scrutiny.

What she discovered did nothing to lessen her misery, which had taken the physical form of a tight knot lodged permanently behind her breast bone.

There were no flaws to discover—one little flaw would have been nice, Katie thought wistfully. She'd automatically assumed that Nikos's suitable bride would be Greek, so it was slightly shocking to be confronted by a tall, confident redhead with green eyes and a soft Irish accent. Maybe this woman had been beautiful in her twenties; now she looked in her—what…mid-thirties?—the word seemed too insipid to describe her, she was simply stunning!

An intrigued expression flickered across Caitlin's face at the form of address used by the younger woman but she didn't comment.

'Sit down, my dear, you look pale…' she advised, widening her inspection to include the small cramped office before turning to the elderly woman who had announced her. 'Perhaps a cup of tea?'

Katie felt suddenly extremely sick.

'I don't want tea,' she replied, judging it time to re-establish who was actually in charge here.

'No, neither do I,' her visitor revealed. 'But I wanted to be private.' Without being asked she removed a pile of papers from a desk and sat down. 'Do you mind if I'm frank? It would save time.'

'Nikos told you about me, then?'

'That he married you.' Caitlin gave an irritated click of her tongue. 'Eventually. Seven years and he didn't say a word, when he told me…' she shook her head '…I can't tell you what a shock it was.'

'I can imagine.' This might very well be the strangest conversation she would ever have in her life.

'And of course with the timing I knew straight off that he did it for me. If I'd known I'd have never taken the money, of course, but, well, what's done is done.'

'I don't understand. What has Nikos marrying me got to do with you? He married me for money.'

'Money *I* needed.' Caitlin sighed. 'My business was in trouble, I'd foolishly over-extended myself. My marriage was going through a rocky period.'

'You were married?'

'I still am.'

'Does Nikos know?'

Caitlin frowned. 'Look, who do you think I am?'

'The woman Nikos is going to marry.'

A look of understanding swept over Caitlin's face. 'My dear girl,' she laughed. 'I'm Nik's stepmother.'

Katie flushed to the roots of her hair. 'I feel such a fool.'

'Don't be, I'm flattered.' The older woman grinned. 'I went to Nik when I didn't know what else to do. If I'd been declared bankrupt Spyros would never have forgiven me for disgracing the family, and if I'd asked him to bail me out he would have believed what he half believed already—that I'd married him for his money. The result would have been much the same either way—our marriage would have been over.

'Nikos agreed to act for me, he could not go through the normal channels because Spyros would have heard about it. I asked my old friend Harvey to help us and he came up with you, though I swear I didn't know it.'

Katie stared. So now she knew why Nikos had married her. The past, no matter how fascinating, did not alter the present—Nikos wanted a divorce, which was no doubt why Caitlin was here to hurry things along.

'Right, well, I'm seeing my lawyer to get my signatures witnessed in the morning. So you can tell Nikos that he won't have to wait long,' she promised.

'Oh, heavens, no, don't do that!'

Katie looked at her blankly. 'Pardon me?'

The redhead's beautiful face creased in consternation. 'My dear girl,' she began earnestly. 'That's what I'm here to ask you—please don't give Nik a divorce…well, not yet, anyhow.'

The bizarre request made Katie think she must have misheard. 'I don't understand.'

The older woman sighed and tugged the silk scarf from around her neck. 'I'm not surprised,' she mused, allowing the fine material to slip through her long fingers. 'It must seem a very strange request to you, and it's probably desperately inconvenient. Nik tells me you have marriage plans of your own?'

Katie flushed. 'I don't,' she said flatly.

'But Nikos said he'd made it right with your boyfriend?' She shrugged. 'Whatever that might involve?'

'It didn't make it right for me.'

Explaining to Tom that she didn't want to marry him even if he did forgive her had been one of the hardest things she'd ever had to do. She supposed she ought to be grateful to Nikos. He'd been right about one thing: she didn't love Tom—at least, not in the way that would make a good marriage, and Tom himself was in love with a Katie that didn't exist. Marrying Tom would mean trying to be that girl and Katie knew she couldn't do that.

'Is that so?'

'Listen…*kyria*—'

'Caitlin, please call me Caitlin.'

'Listen, I don't want to be rude…but I don't understand why you want to delay the divorce.'

'If you sign Nikos will marry that wretched girl, Livia… there's nothing surer.' In her agitation Caitlin's soft brogue deepened. 'And I'd *never* forgive myself,' she declared, 'if I let him do that without making any push to stop him. She'd be the ruination of the boy and I'm terribly fond of him.'

Katie had gathered that much.

'What I need,' she mused, 'is time to come up with a plan and you could give me that time. I don't suppose you've got any ideas?'

Katie, who had been listening with growing fascination, shook her head vigorously. There was no way she was going to get involved in Caitlin Lakis's machinations, though she couldn't help but feel a certain degree of satisfaction that Nikos's chosen bride didn't meet with universal approval.

'I can see what Nikos meant when he said his stepmother was still an active force in his life.'

'Did he say that? How sweet. You know,' she said slowly with a twinkle in her eyes that had Katie been better acquainted with her would have immediately rung warning bells, 'I've just thought of something that *might*, with a bit of jiggling, work...but it would need your assistance,' she added, looking at Katie speculatively.

'I'm afraid that's not possible. It isn't...why are you looking at me like that?'

'I was just thinking that you don't look like the sort of hard-hearted girl who could abandon a basically sound chap to a life of *mediocrity* with the wrong woman...?'

'Nikos is quite old enough to make his own decisions.' *And leave others to deal with the consequences.*

'Oh, you think I'm an interfering old bag.'

Katie laughed—she had never seen anyone who looked less bag-like.

'Oh, I probably am, but the thing is it wouldn't take much. I'm positive he's already got his doubts, but being a Lakis he's just too damned stubborn to admit it. You are fond of him, aren't you?'

This sly rider made Katie start. She gulped, unable to maintain eye contact with that candid green gaze.

'Maybe more than fond...?'

Katie flushed and got to her feet. 'I'm sorry, I really can't help you,' she said stiffly.

Caitlin rose too. 'I'm sorry,' she admitted frankly. 'But think about it, please?' With a winning smile she laid a card down on the table. 'I'm staying here if you want to contact me.' With a smile she turned to go.

'Has Nikos...?'

The older woman turned back.

Katie took a deep breath. 'H-has he mentioned me at all?' she asked with what she knew was a pathetically poor attempt at indifference.

'Hardly at all, despite my efforts.'

Katie's chin went up; she was too proud to let the other woman see how deep her words cut... *Why the shock? It's not as if you didn't already know he didn't care about you.*

'Which in itself is revealing, don't you think?'

Katie raised her downcast eyes, startled by the soft words.

Caitlin smiled back at her, a good deal of understanding in her eyes. 'He's also been in the foulest mood imaginable,' she revealed. 'I'm meddling, I know I am, but after all it's because of me he married you in the first place so I feel responsible.'

Katie sighed heavily. She had thought she'd achieved—what did the psychologists call it? Closure...? Yes, that would be right, closure. If nothing else, Caitlin's visit had revealed that her wounds were still very much open!

Georgina, a dazed expression on her face, re-entered the room. 'You must have been *very* nice to her,' she said faintly. 'She gave me this,' she explained, placing a cheque reverently down on the desk.

Katie looked at the amount written in strong, flowing hand and understood why Georgina looked as if she'd been run over by a truck. 'Very generous.'

'You don't think it will bounce, do you?' Georgina asked with sudden anxiety.

'Relax, it definitely won't bounce.' Of that, but not much else, Katie was sure.

Katie closed her eyes; it felt as if they were dropping out of the sky. It obviously hadn't occurred to Caitlin that Katie had never flown in a helicopter before...so how she'd stare if she knew that before today she'd never flown full stop.

Nobody, she reflected ruefully, could ever have had such a luxurious introduction to air travel. First the private jet to Athens and now Spyros Lakis's personal helicopter, which was just now hovering above the helipad of his yacht—the reason Katie had her eyes closed.

No wonder she was experiencing a sense of unreality.

It was barely forty-eight hours before that she'd rung Caitlin to say that she would go along, but only because she wanted to speak to Nikos herself.

The older woman had not asked what had brought about this change of heart, but Katie wondered if maybe she suspected the reason. There had been something distinctly knowing about her smile when Katie had refused wine with her meal on the flight over.

There was an inescapable irony in someone who had been so openly contemptuous of people who forgot to take the proper precautions, as she had, finding herself pregnant. Katie didn't think it likely that Nikos would see the joke when she told him. She felt sick again as she contemplated doing so—not telling him had never been an option for her; he deserved to know.

She had no idea how active a part, if at all, he would want to take in his child's life, but she was willing to be reasonable up to a point—that point being she wouldn't have another woman bringing up her child!

CHAPTER TWELVE

THE guest list read like a who's who of the rich and famous. Politicians and media moguls rubbed shoulders with famous faces from the fashion and the entertainment industry. It seemed that when her hosts threw a *small* party on board their yacht, people didn't refuse the invitation.

Katie, introduced by Caitlin as a 'dear family friend', mingled and smiled with the best of them and acted as though it were perfectly normal for her to find herself standing next to someone whose love life had been reported in detail in her newspaper the previous week. Similarly she avoided drawing attention to herself by goggling too obviously at original works of art, the like of which she had only previously seen in art galleries, that lined the walls.

Dressed in one of Caitlin's elegant, deceptively simple creations, her hair twisted in a simple knot on her head, she thought she blended in pretty well, but it seemed not everyone was fooled. Her puzzled eyes were drawn once more to the tall, distinguished-looking figure with a head of distinctive silver hair standing alone—he was still staring at her as he had been since she'd entered the room.

Perhaps, she reflected wryly, it was because she was the only female in the room who wasn't wearing a king's ransom in jewellery around her neck. Katie was wondering if she should confront the rude stranger when from amongst the bright chatter around her she picked out the one name—*Nikos*!

Underneath her expertly applied make-up she went desperately pale. *Pull yourself together, Katie,* she remonstrated sternly, *if you go catatonic at the sound of his name just how are you going to deal with the man in the flesh?*

Always supposing Caitlin was right and he did turn up to-night.

'At least that's what my wife says...'

Katie, who had tuned out of the conversation for a vital thirty seconds, had absolutely no idea what the laughing man beside her had been talking about, but clearly he was waiting for her response.

'I believe frills are *huge* this year!' It was only after she'd delivered this inane observation that she recalled that she was no longer in the company of a fashion editor.

The high-ranking diplomat was too polite to come right out and say she was demented, but he did suddenly remember he needed to be somewhere else.

His hurried departure cleared a channel through the crowd of bodies to the other side of the room, revealing in the process a tall, commanding figure who looked quite unbelievably handsome in a formal dark dinner jacket and black tie. He looked exactly what he was, even down to the obligatory blonde in a low-cut dress who was laughing up at him: a rich, incredibly powerful man who was out of her league.

Despite the blonde's energetic attempts to gain his attention, Nikos's dark, arrogant gaze was locked onto Katie's face. Even at this distance she could feel the strong emotions emanating from his still figure.

Seconds later the opening closed over, concealing his face from view; his dark head was still visible above the throng. Sheer panic engulfed Katie as she desperately tried to keep track of the top of his distinctive glossy dark head as it began to weave in and out of the crowds. Someone jiggled her arm, spilling some of her drink on her dress in the process. During the few precious seconds her attention was distracted she lost him.

This had seemed a good idea—*why, exactly?*

What had seemed the right thing to do when she had been in England suddenly no longer seemed such a crash-hot idea after all. If you believed it was foolish to mess with something that wasn't broken, it therefore followed that it was equally foolish to try and fix something that was smashed to smithereens!

Oh, God!

Every instinct she possessed was telling her to run. It was only the knowledge that Caitlin had gone to a great deal of expense to engineer this scene, and of course the fact there wasn't any place for her to hide that he wouldn't track her down to, that held her back.

Caitlin has done her bit, now it's my turn. She had planned what she'd say, practised it down to the last intonation so many times she was word perfect, but now at the vital moment her mind was a perfect blank!

Nervously she lifted her glass to her lips only to discover it was empty; the contents were now a stain on the silky silver-grey fabric of her dress.

'Thank you, but actually I was drinking mineral water,' she began as her glass was almost instantaneously filled by an efficient waiter.

With a smile she looked up to discover it was not a waiter standing there with a bottle of champagne in his hand; the air rushed from her lungs in a silent sigh.

'Oh!'

Unnoticed by either party, Katie's wineglass emptied itself onto the thick carpet and then slipped from her fingers.

'Hello, Nikos.'

Nikos, never one for the polite formalities, just stared at her. Unblinkingly his densely lashed eyes moved over her face examining each minute detail with a fierce air of preoccupation. At least it gave Katie the perfect excuse to stare back. She hadn't appreciated until this moment just how hungry she'd been for the sight of him.

Everything in her came awake as she looked at him; it was as if while they'd been apart even the colours in her life had been muted. The world with him in it was a more vibrant, exciting place. Her pulses leapt; he was so terribly, heartbreakingly beautiful, her throat ached, desire tightened her stomach muscles as her eyes ate him up.

Her chin firmed. No, she'd been right to come. She had to let him decide if he wanted to be part of the life they'd created. This way she'd know one way or the other.

Still he didn't say anything.

Unable to bear the tension another second, Katie spoke. 'Aren't you going to ask me what I'm doing here?' she asked throatily.

Katie saw his chest lift—a signal that he'd started breathing again? His eyes burned like silver flames into hers, then he smiled. It was not a safe, cosy smile; it was a pulse-racing, dangerous version.

'No.'

The motion was so swift and fluid, him covering the space that separated them and then taking her by the shoulders seemed one single, seamless action. His fingers dug into her flesh as they tightened against her collar-bones; Katie barely registered the pain. Standing this close she could hear the echo of his rapid heartbeat…or maybe it was her own? And feel the fine tremors that were rippling through his tense, greyhound-lean frame.

'You're real,' she heard him breathe. 'I thought I was dreaming again.'

He took hold of her chin between his thumb and forefinger and tilted it upwards. His fierce gaze demanded answers, but Katie wasn't attempting to hide anything! This wasn't the place she would have chosen to go public with her feelings, but she doubted she could have disguised them even if she had wanted to!

This wasn't about disguising her feelings to save face, this was about confronting Nikos with them, and if the result was humiliation at least she'd have the comfort of knowing she'd made the attempt.

They were meant to be together—every fibre of her being

told her this. She was a one-man woman and Nikos was that man. But she was also well aware that things that were meant to be didn't always happen.

Still holding her eyes with his, he took her face between his hands and sealed his mouth to hers. The raw hunger in him was overwhelming; at the instant of contact her body went limp. But at the first smooth, stabbing incursion of his tongue between her parted lips the life flowed hotly back into her limbs.

The wave of sexual energy that surged through her body blasted away all remnants of submissiveness and transformed her from a passive to a very active participant in the kiss.

A lost cry vibrated in her throat as she wrapped her arms about his neck and pressed herself sinuously up against him, revelling in the hard, virile strength of his marvellous body.

The abrupt separation when he tore his mouth from hers made Katie feel cold and empty inside. She soon heated up, however, when the significance of the silence in the room, which moments before had been filled with the hum of laughter and voices, struck her.

She wanted the floor to open up and swallow her. All those people watching…speculating, thinking God knew what… Well, actually she could hazard a pretty accurate guess what they were thinking! That was the trouble.

Nikos took one look at her burning face and muttered a low imprecation. He bent his head towards her and spoke in a voice for her ears only.

'You look like a paralysed chicken,' he informed her cruelly. 'Lift your head up! Show some pride. I will not permit you to cower.'

Not permit. 'Just how exactly are you going to stop me?' she gritted. It was all right for him—he was used to having his every action scrutinised in the media and he didn't give a damn what people thought about him.

Nikos met her indignant glare with a smile of dazzling brilliance. 'That's much better,' he approved warmly. He threw his arm about her shoulders and pulled her to his side. 'I think we will continue this conversation somewhere a little less public.'

'Pity you didn't think about that before you kissed me.'

'I didn't think full stop before I kissed you,' he informed her sardonically.

'This is a nice room.'

'My father's study,' Nikos said without taking his eyes from her delicate profile.

'Won't he mind?' she wondered, running her finger along the spine of a leather-bound volume on the bookshelf. 'This looks old.'

'It's a first edition,' Nikos snapped dismissively.

Katie's hand dropped away from the no-doubt priceless book. First editions, old masters on the walls—this place was like a floating museum with Jacuzzis. The disparity between their backgrounds had never been more apparent to her.

'Where is Tom?'

Katie, her lips still tender and swollen from the unbridled passion of his kiss, the taste of him still in her mouth, turned to stare at him incredulously. Of all the things for him to say! Anger started to build inside her…it escalated quickly.

'Why, did you fancy a threesome?'

Nikos's nostrils flared as he inhaled sharply. 'I do not like it when you speak that way,' he told her austerely.

'How fortunate I care so passionately about what you like and dislike,' she replied sarcastically. The simple declaration of love she had intended to make before her confession was fast becoming a distant memory. 'I think the time to wonder if Tom was around might have been before you mauled me in front of all those people, not after!'

Nikos, his hard cheekbones ridged with dull red, hardly heard what she said; he was recalling how very much she had cared once about what he liked…in fact she had begged him to tell her…to instruct her… She had been a very apt pupil.

'Oh, sorry, was I not supposed to mention you just mauled me?'

'I *kissed* you and you gave every indication of liking it.' His eyes darkened. 'Liking it very much,' he added with throaty satisfaction. 'Tom is not here?' he persisted.

His vague tone and inability to grasp a fairly obvious fact suggested his razor-sharp wits were not working at full capacity.

Katie gave a snort of exasperation, lifted a cushion from one of the sofas and made an elaborate show of looking behind it. 'Tom?' She dropped it and turned back, her expression scornful. 'Nope, it looks like he's not,' she added crisply, then, in a sickly syrupy tone, 'Is your fiancée? I'm just *dying* to meet her…'

'Being facetious does not suit you, either,' he observed harshly. His long-lashed eyes narrowed. 'But that dress does.' He swallowed and tore his eyes from her supple curves. 'What *are* you doing here, Katerina?'

She widened her eyes innocently. 'Where else should a woman be but beside her husband?'

'I was wondering why you had not returned the divorce papers…?'

'Oh, I'm a great believer in the personal touch,' she told him grimly. 'Hand delivery.'

'Do you want me to speak to Tom again?' If he wasn't exactly holding his breath, Katie got the impression her reply mattered to him. 'I thought,' he continued when she remained silent, 'I had made him see…'

'See what? That your leftovers were acceptable? That a quick tumble doesn't mean anything? I'd have loved to be a fly on the wall for that tête-à-tête.'

Nikos's face darkened, he loosened his tie and pushed his clenched fists into his pockets. 'I will speak to him again,' he announced distantly, 'if you wish.' Again the penetrating scrutiny.

Was that what he thought she wanted to hear…? *You are such a stupid man!* Katie took a deep breath and forced herself to unclench her fists.

'No need. Tom,' she admitted, 'was *very* understanding. My shameless behaviour was all a reaction to the trauma of almost being killed in the fire.'

'But you are not together?' For a man who had gone out of his way to bring that about, he sounded quite extraordinarily pleased by her solitary state. Looking a lot less tense, he slipped the buttons of his jacket.

Katie trained her eyes on a point beyond his shoulder to stop them straying to the fascinating dark shadow of body hair clearly visible through the fine fabric of his white shirt.

'Perhaps,' she suggested bitterly, 'I don't want to marry a man who is *understanding* when he finds me in bed with his friend? Call me strange, but I don't think it would be healthy to think about another man when my husband was making love to me.'

A white line appeared around Nikos's lips; with an attitude of seething frustration caused by the knowledge he had actually made it possible, he pushed his fingers deep into his hair.

'You slept with Tom?'

'You look annoyed, Nikos,' she observed mildly—actually he looked incandescent with rage. 'A little bit perverse, don't you think? Wasn't I supposed to sleep with Tom?' She shook her head and pretended bewilderment. 'I mean, you went to such great lengths to smooth things over for me it seemed the least I could do.'

'Do not speak like a tart…'

'Why not? You treat me like one.'

'If you speak to me like that you must expect to face the consequences…Katerina,' he warned her.

'I'm trembling…' Every time you touch me. 'Male arrogance,' she told him, shaking her head in disbelief, 'is always a reliable form of entertainment. Good luck to you if you can convince Tom to take your leftovers off your hands. Unfortunately this particular reject doesn't want to be passed around like a piece of merchandise. I don't need you or anyone else to make excuses for me! I'm prepared to live with the consequences of my actions…' Would he? That was the big question.

Nikos strode over to the other side of the room, his hand pressed to his pleated brow. He swung back, a strange expression on his face. 'You said that if you married Tom you would think of another man when your husband made love to you…' he quoted with deadly accuracy.

I knew it was too good to be true that he hadn't noticed that one. 'I don't remember what I said.'

'I do. Would this man by any chance be me, Katerina?' he charged huskily.

'You really do think a lot of yourself, don't you?'

'As I am the only man who has made love to you,' he reminded her with a palpable air of smug male complacency, 'it seems a logical conclusion.'

'How do you know I wasn't thinking of someone else when you were making love to me?'

Nikos threw back his head and laughed, perfectly secure in the knowledge, *and with good reason*, that in the bedroom he could wipe the thought of every other man from a woman's mind.

Her shoulders slumped in defeat.

'Oh, all right, then, I wasn't.'

'Before we go any farther I think we should establish why you are here.' Katie found that, now the moment had arrived, she couldn't say it—she just couldn't… *You're scared of his reaction,* she accused herself. *You're a coward.* 'I repeat, why are you here? I demand an answer.'

Demand was the word that did it. Katie saw red. 'That's your problem, you don't ask nicely,' she taunted angrily.

Nikos's face darkened. An errant muscle in his lean cheek jerked as his jaw tightened to breaking-point. Katie watched these danger signs with a strange sense of objectivity. Another little push and he would snap. Briefly she recklessly toyed with the idea of supplying the requisite pressure, but sense prevailed.

'All right, if you must know Caitlin invited me.'

Nikos shook his head. '*What…?* No,' he said positively. 'That is not possible, you do not know Caitlin.'

'I do now. We met quite recently. She told me why you married me,' she added casually.

Nikos stiffened. 'She should not have done that.'

'No, you should have.'

'I don't suppose she told you that my brother engineered her plight?' He saw Katie's confusion and nodded. 'No, she would not. Dimitri, my brother, always resented Caitlin—he didn't like to share our father with anyone.'

'Including you?'

Nikos looked at her sharply. 'Including me,' he agreed slowly. 'He was too clever to come right out and bad-mouth Caitlin, but he had a way of implying things…'

'And if you imply often enough people start to wonder…?'

'You've got the picture. As for the companies that suddenly called in her loans—he'd hidden his tracks well, but Dimitri was behind that too.'

Katie shuddered; the dead brother sounded a sinister person.

'So you see my brother created the problem.'

'And you felt it was your duty to make right what your brother had broken, no matter what it cost you.' Katie sighed. She was beginning to see the sort of man Nikos was: a man with strong principles who would protect those he loved no matter what the cost to himself.

'I think you too know about duty? And paying your brother's debts?'

Katie gasped and went pale. 'How?'

Nikos shrugged. 'It is always easy to track money if you know where to look. As for the rest, I could only theorise.'

Katie closed her eyes—he knew.

'Your brother was very young.'

Katie blinked back tears and nodded. Nikos was looking at her not with scorn as she had feared, but with warmth and compassion.

'He couldn't live with knowing what he'd done,' she admitted. She discovered it was actually a relief after all these years to be able to speak of it with someone, especially someone who didn't seem to be judging Peter.

'And he left you all alone to fix the harm he had done. My poor Katerina…'

'I don't want your pity, Nikos.'

'That isn't what I want to give you.'

She waited with bated breath for him to expand on this infuriatingly ambiguous statement. When he remained silent she said the first thing that came into her head.

'And your father is a dear, isn't he?' Actually calling Spyros Lakis a 'dear' was a bit like calling a lion cute, but despite all her preconceptions she had warmed to the strong, silent man who was clearly besotted by his wife.

Nikos was regarding her with an expression of reluctant fascination. 'You have met my father?' The significance of her presence appeared to finally hit him. 'You are a guest here, on the yacht?'

'Well, I'm not a stowaway.' Katie placed her hands on her slim hips and stuck her chin out. 'And I'm not leaving!' she declared belligerently. 'I'm here as a guest of your parents whether you like it or not and I'll go when they ask me to leave and not before.'

'Did I say I wanted you to go?'

'No, but—'

'But nothing.' Nikos folded his arms across his chest. 'What crazy scheme has Caitlin got you involved in?'

He clearly knew his stepmother pretty well. 'She is unhappy about your plans to marry this…Livia. She asked me not to sign the papers to give her time to…'

'Interfere,' Nikos supplied drily.

Katie was deeply confused by his sudden relaxed almost mellow attitude. He hadn't struck her as the sort of man who took people interfering in his life lightly.

'So you didn't sign the papers.' His eyes narrowed. 'But that doesn't explain your presence here.'

Katie grimaced. 'I wanted to see how the other half live,' she responded flippantly.

'And is it the way you imagined?'

'I feel a little out of my depth,' she admitted.

Nikos reached across and ran his finger over her rounded chin. 'You have nothing to prove to anyone. Remember that,' he instructed, looking deep into her startled face. 'Now why did you really come?'

'I think Caitlin thought I might be able to…*distract* you.'

There was a long, nerve-stretching silence.

'Very delicately put,' Nikos observed slowly.

'Don't worry, I didn't agree. Don't panic.' Pretty ironic advice considering he looked cool and collected and she was about ready to fall to pieces. 'I'm not here to seduce you, Nikos.'

'I feel better already,' he revealed with no discernible inflection in his deep, dry voice.

'You're a grown man quite capable of deciding who you want to spend the rest of your life with.'

'Rest of my life?' An odd expression flickered across his stony countenance.

'Well, that's what marriage is about, isn't it?' she said crossly. 'You must have thought about that.'

'As you no doubt did when you accepted Tom's proposal,' he countered slyly.

Lips tight, Katie flicked back her long silky hair and fixed him with an unfriendly look. 'You can marry who you like, but it might not be so easy after…you know…'

'I know what?'

An irritated grunt emerged from her lips. Even the most besotted and liberal of girlfriends was not likely to view her future husband passionately kissing a strange woman with equanimity. A dreamy, distracted expression drifted into her eyes…it was passionate wasn't it…?

'Well, don't you think that maybe it would be a good idea for you to go and explain to Livia about the…you know…*kissing thing*?' Her eyes, stinging with tears, slid from his.

Virtue might be its own reward but she had yet to see the proof. Katie cursed the wretched sense of fair play that made her act as an advocate for the enemy.

'And say what exactly?' His predatory expression made her stomach flip. 'That I saw you, and could think of nothing but tasting you, feeling your body beneath me…'

'Nikos?' she gasped.

'Do not look at me like that, *yineka mou* or I shall not be responsible,' he warned huskily. 'I will not explain to Livia because she did not see me kiss you.'

'I saw…'

'Not Livia.' Nikos dismissed the blonde with a click of his fingers. 'Even if she had seen me I would still not explain. Livia and I decided we would not suit after all,' he revealed smoothly.

'I'm sorry.'

He grinned. 'You are a delightful but most unconvincing liar. Now tell me, if you are not here to seduce me…a bitter blow,' he admitted solemnly, 'why are you here?'

'It's just there's something I thought you should know…'

'Something so important that you had to tell me face to face?'

Katie nodded.

'It can't be that bad.'

'You'll probably think it is.' She felt it only fair to warn him. 'I just thought you might want to know that you're going to be a father.'

He froze. *'Father…?'* he repeated in a strangled voice. 'Might!' he added in an even stranger tone.

'Nikos!' she wailed, deeply alarmed by the grey tinge of his skin. 'Maybe you should sit down.'

'I'm not the one who is pregnant,' he gritted back.

Katie was relieved to see he had recovered some of his colour. 'I didn't mean to blurt it out like that, honestly. And before you say anything I'm not here to ask for anything,' she added fiercely. 'I just thought that you should know about the baby.'

'You are carrying my child.' His eyes dropped to her flat belly. *'Theos…!'* He clasped a hand to his head. 'Why did I not think of this?' His face hardened with self-reproach that Katie read as anger.

'I'm really sorry, but…'

'You are sure?'

Katie jerked back, her expression indignant. 'Of course I'm sure! Do you really think I'd have said anything if I wasn't?'

Nikos, who appeared to be deep in thought, nodded absently, not seeming to notice her resentment.

'And you have seen a doctor, of course.'

'Not yet,' she admitted. 'But I did two tests and they're accurate,' she added in face of his accusing expression.

'I will arrange for us to see a doctor first thing tomorrow.'

'He'll only say the same thing, Nikos.' He was clearly still clinging to the hope that she was mistaken, she thought, irrationally saddened by his attitude.

'I don't doubt it, but the sooner you receive proper medical care the better.'

'I'm not ill, I'm pregnant.'

'With my child, Katerina…' He dragged a hand shakily through his hair. 'My child is growing inside you,' he groaned wonderingly.

'You're not angry…?'

He looked at her as if she were mad. *'Angry?'*

'Well, this is hardly the sort of news that you want to celebrate.'

'Is that the way you feel?' he demanded tautly.

Katie felt it was significant he'd avoided answering her question. 'Well,' she admitted, wryly, 'I was pretty freaked when I realised.'

'You were alone,' Nikos recognised in a strained undertone.

'But now I kind of like the idea,' she explained with a self-conscious smile. 'It must have something to do with maternal instincts and all that,' she added, a defensive note creeping into her voice.

Nikos nodded. 'I ''kind of like the idea'' too.'

'That's nice of you,' she replied with a watery smile. 'It really is.' She sniffed. 'But you don't have to pretend.'

An expression of extreme exasperation crossed Nikos's face. 'I am not being kind or pretending. And I do not wish to hear you speak again of our baby as if it is some unwanted burden. Do you think me so incapable of the same feelings you claim for yourself?'

Katie shook her head, bewildered by the deep emotions throbbing in his voice. 'You want this baby?' She gasped.

'Did I not say so?'

'No, as a matter of fact you didn't.'

A brief smile flickered across his face. 'Well, for the record, I am happy. Did you tell Caitlin?'

Katie shook her head. 'I didn't, but she might suspect,' she admitted.

Nikos nodded. 'Do you want a big wedding?'

CHAPTER THIRTEEN

KATIE'S knees sagged and Nikos, his eyes fixed with alarm on her milk-pale face, scooped her up as if she were a child, and, ignoring her weak protests, placed her down on a sofa.

Katie would have sat up if a firm hand on her chest had not prevented her. 'I'm fine.'

'You have clearly been overexerting yourself,' he accused. 'You weigh nothing.'

'I'm being careful, I'm not stupid. It's just that...for a minute there I thought you said *wedding*!' From some hidden reserve she dredged a weak laugh.

'Naturally we will get married—anything else is unacceptable.'

'We are married,' she reminded him.

'Maybe on paper,' he admitted with a dismissive grimace. 'But I want to do the thing properly this time...a priest, a church...'

'People do not get married because they are having a baby, Nikos.' *They get married because they love one another,* she thought bleakly. It had not escaped her notice that love was a subject that Nikos was steering clear of. A loveless marriage, could she bear it? What was the alternative?

'Here they do,' he corrected her drily. 'I am Greek and so is my father. He is a proud man, and strong traditionalist—he would not accept a civil ceremony,' he explained glibly. 'If I produced a bastard he would disown me and he would die of shame...possibly literally. You know, of course,' he added, 'that he had two severe heart attacks a few years ago, and has undergone bypass surgery.'

'So what you're saying is that if I don't marry you I'll be responsible for your father's death?'

Nikos gave a fatalistic shrug.

'No undue pressure, then,' she breathed shakily.

'And our child might be considered an outcast,' he added brutally.

'That's so cruel!' Katie found it impossible to match his pragmatic manner.

Nikos brushed a strand of hair from her eyes. 'I do not make the rules.'

'But you live by them,' she accused.

His finger trailed lightly down the soft curve of her jaw. 'You will marry me...?'

Katie turned her cheek into his cupped palm and gave a sigh. 'It would be a disaster,' she predicted, blinking as her eyes filled with hot tears—Nikos hated tears.

She started when his finger found a single drop of salty moisture on her cheek. He touched it and then he raised his damp finger to his lips and touched his tongue to it.

Katie's insides melted like warm honey as she stared transfixed by the earthy, erotic spectacle.

He framed her face with his hands. 'I will not make you cry,' he promised fiercely.

The emotions she heard in his deep voice moved her once more to tears.

'You already make me break my promise,' he chided huskily. 'I think I shall have to kiss you better? Unless you have a better idea.'

Katie sniffed, trying not to listen to the voice in her head that was calling her a weak fool. *What happened to proudly confronting him with your true feelings, Katie...?*

'I don't,' she admitted with a sniff.

The driver who was sitting in the back of the air-conditioned limo jumped out startled when he saw her approach.

'I'm sorry, I understood you would not need the car for another hour.'

'I won't need it at all,' she told him sunnily. 'I need to go into the city. Don't worry, I'll catch a bus and go from there to meet Mr Lakis.'

'Catch a bus?' the driver echoed with as much horrified shock as if she'd just announced her intention of robbing a bank.

'Could you tell me where this is?' she asked, showing the address written on the note she'd discovered when she'd returned to her stateroom earlier that morning. 'Is this place far from where I'm to meet Mr Lakis?'

The driver confirmed it was in fact within walking distance, so Katie set off with mixed feelings for her assignation.

The short note had revealed its author to be the silver-haired man who had been watching her so intently. He had apologised for offending her and gone on to explain he had been a friend of her mother and he recognised her from the snapshots of her Eleri had sent him when she was a child.

Katie was eager to meet someone who had known her mother; the details she had of Eleri's earlier life were meagre. It didn't even cross her mind to refuse the suggestion that she meet this man in a café before lunch. She could meet him and then go on to meet Nikos as arranged.

She reached the café a little before the arranged time; the silver-haired stranger who had identified himself as Vasilis Atmatzidis was sitting in a corner, and he rose to his feet when he saw her.

'Mr Atmatzidis...?' she said, holding out her hand.

'Vasilis,' he said, taking her hand and raising it with old-fashioned gallantry to his lips.

Katie looked at him curiously. Despite the silver hair she judged him to be in his early to mid forties. Slim and a little above average height, he was extremely good-looking.

'I think I annoyed you last night,' he said after ordering

coffee for them both. 'I was just so surprised to see you there of all places…'

'I wondered why you seemed familiar,' Katie said suddenly. 'You were at the funeral, weren't you?' Her memories of the day were pretty confused but she did recall a well-dressed stranger who nobody had seemed to know who had stood at the back of the church and left without speaking to anyone. 'And it must have been you who sent the flowers with the card written in Greek.'

Vasilis nodded. 'I thought of approaching you, but Eleri always said that you got upset if she mentioned anything about her life in Greece.'

'I got angry. They treated my mother terribly.'

The older man sighed. 'Your grandfather was a proud, stubborn man,' he admitted. 'He missed her terribly, you know.'

'Well, I hope he suffered as much as she did,' Katie responded honestly. She was not inclined to forgive and forget. 'How did you know my mother?'

'I was the man she was meant to marry.'

Katie's eyes went round with astonishment. '*You!* And you stayed friends…?'

'I valued your mother's friendship and once my heart and pride healed we corresponded regularly, and several times when I came to London we met up. She was always eager for news of old friends.'

'I think she was homesick sometimes,' Katie said quietly.

'Perhaps, but she never regretted her decision; she loved your father very much.'

Katie felt the prick of tears behind her eyelids. 'Tell me about her,' she asked huskily. 'Tell me about what she was like when she was young.'

Vasilis was an entertaining raconteur and soon Katie was laughing out loud as, with a roguish gleam in his eyes, he recalled some hair-raising exploits.

'I don't believe she did that!' Katie exclaimed after he recounted one particular episode.

'It's true,' he promised. 'I swear.' The laughter died from his eyes as they swept over her face. 'You know, when you laugh you look like her.'

Impulsively Katie caught his hand and squeezed. 'Did you ever marry?'

'No, he never married.'

Katie started at the sound of a very familiar voice. 'Nikos!' Her welcoming smile faded as she encountered the shimmering hostility in Nikos's rigid face.

Dismayed and alarmed, she watched as he took a swaggering step forward and wedged his thigh up against her chair so that even had she wanted to leave she couldn't have.

'And the reason Vasilis has never married,' he continued loudly, 'is that he is a womaniser, who prefers quantity to quality.'

The look he gave the other man made Katie cringe on his behalf. Anyone would think from the way he was acting he wanted to pick a fight.

'You two know one another, I take it,' Katie said drily. She still didn't have the faintest idea why Nikos was acting so obnoxiously.

'Oh, yes,' Vasilis agreed. 'I've known Nikos since he was a baby.'

'Playing the experience card is calculated risk, Vasilis. There's always the danger that the lady in question will realise that you're old enough to be her father.' The older man's appreciative laughter seemed to infuriate Nikos even more. 'We are leaving, Katerina.'

'I'm not going anywhere with you until you apologise to Vasilis. Honestly,' she said to the older man, 'I don't know what's got into him.'

Nikos inhaled through quivering nostrils and released a flood of Greek for the older man's benefit. Katie might not have been able to understand a word of it, but it didn't sound as if it was anything friendly. Halfway through the diatribe Vasilis's mocking smile faded. He looked from Katie to Nikos with startled incredulity.

'You are married, Katie?' he asked when Nikos had subsided into silent hostility.

'Sort of,' she admitted. 'It's a long story.'

'*Sort of* was enough to get you pregnant,' Nikos reminded her.

'I thought you didn't want the world to know before you told your parents.'

'Don't worry, your secret is safe with me,' Vasilis promised, getting to his feet. He bowed to Katie. 'Until we meet next time, my dear.'

'I'd like that.' Katie smiled, turning her back pointedly on Nikos. You couldn't really blame the older man for leaving—Nikos did look pretty scary.

Not that she was scared. On the surface this seemed a foolish response, but when she analysed it she realised that she knew deep down that Nikos would never hurt her. Whatever else changed in her life this wouldn't; she would always be safe with him.

'If there's a next time,' Nikos informed Vasilis with a belligerent growl, 'I'll break your damned neck. Just keep away from my wife!'

Vasilis seemed to take this threat in good part. Katie was less tolerant.

'How could you?' she breathed wrathfully as the other man left.

Nikos pulled a wad of notes from his pocket and slammed them on the table. 'Let's get out of here.'

'I'm not going anywhere with you.'

'You can leave on your own two feet or slung over my shoulder. The choice,' he announced generously, 'is yours.'

Katie examined his grim face; she decided he wasn't bluffing. 'I'm going because I want to.'

'Of course you are.'

'And I hate you.'

'We'll discuss your feelings for me later.'

The fifteen-minute journey to his apartment building was completed in silence, the sort of silence that made the air-conditioning redundant.

If Nikos's temper had cooled by the time the door of his apartment had closed her own had peaked.

'I accept that there was no deception on your part and I am prepared to make allowances for your inexperience, but you have to promise me never again to go anywhere near Vasilis.'

'I will do no such thing and how dare you tell me who I may and may not have as a friend? You behaved like a thug,' she condemned severely. 'I've never been so embarrassed in my life!'

Nikos surveyed her angry, flushed face with outraged eyes. 'I behaved…' His chest swelled. 'I behaved with incredible restraint considering the provocation!' he bellowed. 'If I'd done to that *man* what I wanted to you might have room for complaint. How did you expect me to act? I come back early and find my wife has gone off to meet the most notorious womaniser in the country and she hasn't even had the decency to hide it from me. My own chauffeur told me!'

'Fine, next time I have an assignation I'll lie my head off. Will that make you happy?'

Nikos grabbed her by the shoulders and jerked her to him. 'There won't be a next time,' he ground. 'Because I'm not going to let you out of my sight. *Theos!*' he groaned. 'Why are you doing this to me?'

Her soft heart couldn't take the sort of anguish she recognised in his face. 'I went to meet Vasilis because he knew my mother.'

'Is that what he told you?' Nikos laughed harshly. 'Look,

I know women find him attractive and he's a very plausible guy, but—'

'No, *really*, he knew my mother. He was to be married to her, but she ran away with my father.'

'No, that can't be right. Vasilis was betrothed to the Kapsis girl.'

'My mother.'

Nikos looked dumbfounded. 'Your mother was Michalis Kapsis's daughter…?'

Katie nodded. 'Her family disowned her when she married my father. He wasn't good enough for them,' she recalled bitterly.

'And you have never had any contact with them?'

Katie shook her head.

'This is extraordinary—*Theos*!' he exclaimed suddenly. 'This Greek you taunted me with—the one you lived with—it was your mother,' he breathed.

Katie nodded.

'You are half Greek.'

'I've been trying all my life to forget that…'

Nikos pulled her into the circle of his arms and Katie laid her head against his chest. The hand that stroked her hair suddenly stilled.

'I made a total fool of myself.'

'Yes, you did.' She lifted her head. 'Why did you, Nikos?' Her eyes widened in astonishment as he blushed—he actually blushed!

'Well, I wanted to protect you as any husband would—' He broke off and took a deep breath. 'No, I acted like that because I was insane with jealousy.'

'You were jealous?'

'I am jealous of every man who looks at you. I love you, *pethu mou*, I've known it since that first night, but I wouldn't admit it even to myself. I was so sick at the thought of you going back to Tom that I invited him up to the room. It was despicable and everything you said was right…that's why I tried to make things right between you, I thought I would do the noble thing. I told myself that you being happy was what mattered and if you were happy with Tom then so be it. I think noble is overrated. I went through seven sorts of hell thinking of you with him,' he said hoarsely.

'You love me…' she echoed, still trying to absorb the astonishing things he'd said. 'But why,' she demanded with a groan, 'didn't you tell me? I've been so miserable.'

'Coping with the pregnancy alone?'

'No, sleeping alone, stupid!' she told him lovingly. Clearly he was going to need it spelling out. Her voice dropped a husky octave. 'I love you,' she spelt out, looking up at her incredibly gorgeous husband with shining eyes. 'That's why I let Caitlin bring me here. I decided I had to tell you, but I chickened out at the last minute,' she admitted. 'Because I thought you only wanted to marry me for the baby.'

Nikos's eyes blazed like beacons of love. 'The baby is a bonus,' he said huskily as he gathered her into his arms.

Katie threw him a sultry smile. 'You know, I never did get any lunch.'

'And you are hungry?'

'Always when I look at you,' she admitted simply.

The wedding went like a dream and Nikos had promised her the honeymoon would be even better. Katie, who had learnt her husband always delivered on his promises, saw no reason to disbelieve him.

Katie was sitting wrapped in a golden glow of contentment and not much else besides a few scraps of lace, her wedding gown lying on the bed beside her, when Nikos walked in.

'You make a very provocative picture.'

'Want to do something about it?' she asked with a saucy

smile. Before he could reply she saw the gift-wrapped parcel in his hand. 'A wedding present?'

Nikos nodded. 'From me to you,' he said, handing it to her.

'Why, thank you.' She smiled, tearing the wrapping paper.

Nikos watched her enthusiasm with a proud, tender smile. 'I hope you like it.'

Katie had revealed a leather-bound book. It lay on her knee for a moment before she opened it. 'This is…' Her entire body stiffened as she saw what lay within. She raised tear-filled eyes to Nikos's face before returning eagerly to the contents of the book.

She cried out in wonder every so often as she pored over the pages and by the time she finished she was openly sobbing.

She placed the leather-bound volume reverently down on the bed and ran across to her husband, who folded her in a rib-cracking embrace.

'I thought I'd lost them for ever. I don't know how you did it…' she sniffed emotionally '…but thank you, a million times thank you.'

'It wasn't so hard,' he insisted modestly. 'I contacted friends, the local newspaper had some of Petros when he was swimming competitively, but it was Vasilis who really helped. Your mother had sent him a number of snaps of you and Petros over the years and he had lots of snaps of your mother when she was young.'

'Yes, I've not seen some of them before.' She touched the side of his face with her hand. 'You do know that you are a lovely, *lovely* man, don't you?'

'Shall we keep that between you and me? It is not an asset in the business world for it to be known one has a heart.'

'Nobody needs to know what goes on behind closed doors…' she agreed huskily.

His eyebrows lifted. 'That then leaves us free to do…?'

'Almost anything we want,' Katie completed smoothly. 'Got any ideas?'

'Well, actually…' Katie began. Her eyes twinkled. 'Can I whisper this?'

Nikos obligingly bent his head. 'You know something,' he said when she had finished. 'You are a very bad woman.'

'No, I'm *your* very bad woman. For better—' she sighed happily, tugging at his tie '—or worse.'

Leaving aside the worse part, Katie didn't think it could get much better than being married to Nikos. And as she took him by the hand and led him to the bed she told him so.

MILLS & BOON

Modern Romance™

A PASSIONATE MARRIAGE *by Michelle Reid*

Hot-Blooded Husbands... Greek tycoon Leandros Petronades married Isobel on the crest of a wild affair. But within a year the marriage crashed and burned. Three years on, Leandros comes face to face with Isobel again and finds their all-consuming mutual attraction is as strong as ever...

THE MARRIAGE TRUCE *by Sara Craven*

The bridesmaid's in love – with the best man! Jenna is happy to be her cousin's bridesmaid, but she wishes someone had warned her that the best man is dynamic Ross Grantham – the man she once exchanged marriage vows with in the very same church!

KEEPING LUKE'S SECRET *by Carole Mortimer*

Carole Mortimer's 115th book! When Leonie meets the enigmatic Luke Richmond he takes an instant dislike to her, and repeatedly asks her to leave. But he's hiding something and Leonie's not going anywhere until she finds out more...

THE PARISIAN PLAYBOY *by Helen Brooks*

Getting down to business in the boardroom – and the bedroom! When Jacques Querruel decided he wanted shy Holly Stanton as his personal secretary, Holly fully intended not to be swept off her feet. But being whisked away to Jacques's Paris penthouse, working long hours by his side, she was bombarded with temptation!

On sale 7th February 2003

Available at most branches of WH Smith, Tesco, Martins, Borders, Eason, Sainsbury's and all good paperback bookshops.

1202/01a